Ophelia Bloom

By Coral Cooper

This book is for people who can relate to book one. I love you.

Trigger warning

This book may be triggering to some readers.
There is always someone who wants to help you,
you are not alone. You are loved.

Chapter 1

"Are you okay?" Cole's hand finds the bottom of my exposed back from where my top has been riding up, my muffin top on show, steadying me as he walks past me. Arching my back, trying to keep any balance I have left after carrying a bowling ball around inside me. Feeling her kick and punch letting me know that it's time to sit down.

"I'm okay." I say with a hand on my hip, the other still clinging to the tape gun. Which I'm not sure how came to my possession but I'm grateful from it right now. Cole made me *very* aware that I was to do no heavy lifting of any kind and my tasks were to be confined to taping up boxes and 'looking pretty'. I don't know how anyone can look pretty eight months pregnant. I look like a mix of a beached whale and big foot.

I remember when I moved into this flat. I was eighteen, single, heartbroken and looking back on it, a hot mess. Now I'm twenty-two, engaged, pregnant and… I was going to say put together, but moving at eight months pregnant seems like someone who is a hot mess would do. Let's say I'm less of a hot mess than I was before, that seems like an improvement.

Me and Cole have been together for three and half years now. And I wouldn't change a single second of it. Well maybe that's a lie. I would change a lot of things, like I would have met his parents sooner, like we probably shouldn't have waited until we got engaged. They didn't seem so happy about that. They're also not happy about the fact that we are having our bundle of joy out of wed lock. `It'll be a bastard` his dad exclaimed when we told him. Wait until I tell him that we don't plan on *actually* getting married. I've never wanted to get married; I didn't even want to get engaged. I always told Cole that marriage was off the table. And he was fully understanding but he did say that he wanted some form of commitment. So, we compromised and got 'engaged'. And I wouldn't change that for the world. I had no idea that it was coming, did not expect it in the slightest, it was a complete shock to the system. I just started bawling my eyes out in the middle of the coffee shop, we try our best to make it a weekly thing to go into the coffee shop, our coffee shop, it's our special spot.

When I found out I was pregnant, that was an even bigger shock. I've always felt in tune with my body, my period has always been spot on, always got it in the morning time, then when I woke up that morning and hadn't started my period I ran out to boots and bought a test before Cole woke up. And when that word `pregnant` popped up I screamed, waking Cole up and he ran into the bathroom. That day and every day that I've been pregnant will stay with me forever. The care Cole takes in making sure I'm okay, even more than he did before. He's been at my beck and call. Especially in these past few weeks since I can't tie my own shoes, *single pair of shoes*, none of my shoes fit me, I'm stuck between a pair of Coles old trainers and slippers. Those are the only things that can fit on my feet right now.

As much as I'd love to keep this flat forever, we have well and truly outgrown it. I grip the handrail jiggling the lock for the last time. *Deep breath.* "Thank you." I whisper to the door, before sliding the key under the welcome mat with my swollen feet because there's zero chance of me standing back up if I bend down. It will forever hold a special place in my heart, I found myself here, I found a better version of myself here. The first night I spent here I didn't have any furniture and I deep down was feeling awful. I felt like I had let so many people down. I felt so awful that night that I text the man whose heart I broke wanting forgiveness. I ate my feelings with a Chinese takeaway and got on with my life. But that lonely first night was the first night of the rest of my life.

Cole waits for me at the bottom of the close, holding my handbag for me and holding out his hand for me to hold. "Are you okay?" He whispers. For the second time in the space of ten minutes. I nod. Holding back the tears, I don't know if its happy tears, sad tears, or just plain old pregnancy tears. Cole buckles my seatbelt for me and gently kisses the side of my head. "There you go beautiful." He chimes before leaning down the kiss the bump. I smile every time I see him look, touch or kiss the bump. He is going to be such an amazing dad. I can imagine him now, playing tea parties, and playing at the park just like the child that he is.

I wonder if I'm going to be a good mum though.

What if when it comes to it, I'm not maternal at all? What if I don't know how to be a mum? What if she hates me?

My thoughts are taken over by Cole's hand on mine, squeezing it momentarily before he glances over at me. "I love you." He says before starting the ignition.

"I love you too." I sing back. I'm so fucking glad that I met him. He tosses his head back getting his golden hair out of his eyes. I wonder if our baby will have his hair and eyes. My hair is quite a bit darker than Coles, mines is also wavy. My eyes have more brown in them than Coles, but if the sun hits mine, they have the greenish ness about them that Coles do even when its dark outside.

We have help to move this time. Cole was very stern about that too. Dan and his university friends are getting slipped a few quid and a takeaway to move us in. They're already here when we pull into our street. And I'm suddenly terrified. The fear that I had when I had the urge to move is coming back to me. Even though we're still in Glasgow and are nowhere near the small town I grew up in, I still feel that sense of `homeliness` that seems unfamiliar to me now. I shake away my feelings before we pull into the driveway. Dan drove my car here for me. Because you guessed it, I'm too big to drive, like I literally can't reach the pedals comfortably because I have to sit the seat so far back to not dig into the bump. I can hear the drilling of flat packed furniture and the sound of Lacy delegating. I laugh under my breath as I unclick the seatbelt. Cole's hand finds mine again as he rushes to the passenger side and pulls me from the car.

This is the first time I've been here since we signed the papers. The three-bedroom three-bathroom house is everything I never wanted. When I moved into the flat it felt like mine, this house doesn't feel like mine yet. It feels too cinematic, and too perfect, there's no leaky taps, wonky switches. It's all perfect. The room that I should be most excited about is baby girls room, but I'm more excited about my office. It'll be a huge upgrade from the desk in the living room. I'm working on my second book, I'm in the very beginning stages but it's insane that I create things and I can make a career out of it. I've found a way to put my past and my emotions into something and make a difference in someone's life because of it. And I'm excited to have a room dedicated to it.

Waddling my way along the hallway, Cole following closely behind me. The patio doors displaying the February frost from outside so perfectly. I lean against the marble kitchen island and watch the chaos ensue. Big burly men dumping boxes left, right and centre.

"Stop biting your nails." Cole says, swatting my hand away from my mouth. I didn't even realise I was biting them. "What's wrong?" He twiddles a stray piece of my stray fringe as he turns to face me.

"This is scary." I admit. My eyes find his, he pulls my head into his body and all my tension evaporates.

"I know it's scary. But…I want to give you a life that you deserve." My heart breaks when he says it. I never realised it, but I do deserve it. I deserve a three-bedroom house. I deserve an actual office. I deserve a life with someone I love. I deserve to freak out about it as well.

"Our daughter deserves it too." She deserves a family that loves eachother. She deserves what I didn't have.

"Yeah, she does." He smirks, planting a kiss on top of my head, still with a hand on my French pleated hair. Cole is going to be an amazing dad.

Baby girl kicks me in the ribs when I think about how amazing of a dad he'll be. "Oh, are you missing out on my attention?" He laughs, feeling the pelt through my clothes. Bending down and kissing the bump. "We are going to make this home such a good one for you, my love." His hands rubbing my sides, my hands play with his hair as he admires the bump. He stares up at me. "I love you, Ophelia."

"I love you too Cole."

This home isn't built of bricks and mortar, it is built out of love.

Chapter

2

My contributions to moving and unpacking starts and ends with 'add to cart'. I'm fixating on mine and Cole's bathroom. Probably the room that I should be leaving to the last to decorate, which I think is why I have been enjoying doing it so much. I bought pink stick-on tiles that I have absolutely no intention on actually sticking on. A selection of pink bathroom accessories are getting delivered today.

Cole has been touching up paint upstairs all morning, so I have been shunned to the downstairs. The smell of the paint is driving me crazy, and I won't stop complaining about it. But

Cole says I'm aloud to complain. *Ya know, carrying his baby and all.*

Pulling my laptop onto my lap and plugging in the charger. I've been trying to work on my second book. I've been trying for months now but being pregnant and having zero motivation doesn't help me. My first book was a hit. It still is. I get recognised on the street sometimes. Which is insane. My first book was about self-care and self-love. *Very hypocritical of me I know.* I spent months researching and getting statistics. I realised after I had finished it and finalised all my illustrations for it. That I hadn't taken care of myself the entire time. And now that I *have* been taking care of myself. *Well at least trying to.* I can't find the motivation to start. I don't know what I want the book to be about. All I know is that I'm destined to do this. When I wrote my first book, I had never felt so alive. I locked myself in my apartment for weeks, leaving just to drop off orders and for the odd coffee. I felt like Frankenstein, not Frankenstein's monster. Fun fact Frankenstein was the scientist who created the monster. The monster is called Frankenstein's monster. *Lots of people get it confused.* But anyways I legit felt like a mad scientist, jumbling words together and creating magic. Cole supported me through it. He held me while I cried about what I read, holding me on the couch while I cried tears of sleep deprivation and mania. He would come home from work with a new book to add to the collection and a fun drink for me. He would wake up in the middle of the night to find me, pacing the living room thinking out loud. The book drained me. But I knew that if I wrote it, and even if one person read it, it would help them. I would be able to help someone. The day it got published Cole stayed up all night to make me a cake from scratch. Iced it and everything. I celebrated with a slice of undercooked cake and a shower. The next few weeks were a blur, I signed hundreds of books, had book signing events at local bookshops. I met so many people who claimed that my book changed their lives. And I had never felt so alive, so needed. And yet now I stare at the blank word document craving that feeling again and I don't know how to get it back.

Between our mantel piece where the projector will soon be installed, we have put rows of shelving on either side to house all our books. Well, most of them. The smutty books are in the bedroom of course. I don't think Cole's family would be very happy about that.

Putting my laptop to the side, I take the stacks of books that are creating mini skyscrapers around the living room and try my best to organise them.

Browsing through each book and remembering how it felt when I read it. Me and Cole read together a lot. We haven't read together since moving and all our books have been packed up, but there would be times that we would both want to read the same book so we would take it in turns each reading a chapter out loud. We would get lost in each other's voices and end up kissing. *Especially if we were reading smut.* I don't think Cole ever wanted to read it, but he just knew it would get me all hot and bothered. Nothing like a little fictional foreplay.

Standing on my tippy toes to reach the top shelf where the educational books that are all half read that we have *absolutely* no intention of completing will live. Sprinkling fake plants and nik naks around the shelves to make it look intentionally cluttered. Standing back, checking where to put the next stack.

"Are you having fun?" Cole asks, I spin around, he's standing at the living room entrance leaning his arms against the door frame.

"Yeah." I croak. I admire the stack of books in my arms. "Can we read together?" I ask hopefully, I flash the doe eyes that he can't resist.

He smiles and tilts his head to the floor. "Of course. I'll go make some tea and get some blankets." He twists around and heads for the kitchen.

Sifting through the stack and settling on a cheesy rom com, one that Cole brought home from work one day. The pages still smelling fresh and new.

A few minutes later Cole comes into the living room with a tray of chocolate biscuits and herbal tea, a blanket hanging over his shoulder. Sitting the tray on the coffee table and lying himself down on the couch. I lie on top of him, my back against his stomach as he pulls the blanket around me before I start to read.

He kisses my hair every few minutes before we take turns in reading. It feels just as it felt when we were in my apartment. But even more magical.

Chapter

3

I wake up with a soft kiss from Cole. “Good morning beautiful.” He says as he twirls a piece of my frizzy hair, then planting another kiss on my lips.

“Good morning.” I smile, stretching myself out and bundling the duvet covers under my chin. Somehow, I’ve woke up even more tired than before I went to sleep. I’m looking forward to today. I’m having my last pamper session until bump comes. And I’m excited to get out the house for a few hours. It’s not that I don’t love it. Of course, I do. But everything just seems too good.

I slump myself in the salon waiting area before anyone has a chance to know I'm here. This is my final pamper session before baby girl comes. And I could not be more excited. They don't tell you that pregnancy takes everything from you, your nails. Your skin, your hair, your sex drive. *Man, I don't remember the last time we had sex.* Wait, no it was two months ago and I was so uncomfortable that I just gave up half way through. Cole rolled over, kissed me and said, 'it's okay'. I cried myself to sleep, Cole didn't know though.

"Oh, hello my little darlings." My mum rushes over, eyes to the bump before her eyes get to me. That's another thing about being pregnant, people see a pregnant woman before they see you. It makes you feel like an animal in a zoo. "How are you feeling Lia?" She asks, her attention to me now, her hand rubbing my shoulder.

I bite my tongue when I go to say, 'I'm okay'. That's still one of the habits that I've been trying to break. "I'm at the uncomfortable please get out of me stage." I sigh standing up. Even though I can't wait to meet my daughter and not feel like a beached whale, a part of me wishes she would just stay inside me. Every time I feel her kick me, punch me, every time I hold my bump or look at myself in the mirror, for the first time ever I don't feel alone. I feel like I'm getting a constant hug from the inside. I can imagine her talking to me- 'thank you for eating your greens mummy, thank you for being kind to yourself mummy.' I'm being a lot nicer to myself because she's here, and I want her to be the best person she can possibly be. I want to be the best version of myself, not for me, not for Cole, for her. And if she leaves I'm afraid that I wont be nice to myself.

Laying on the beauty bed, legs spread, having hot wax applied and ripped off of you, doesn't seem like the kind of pamper session that most people look forward to but it's the first time all week that I can relax. Being in the house is stressing me out, and the paint fumes are giving me a headache. I've left Cole alone today. Well, he said his sister was coming over to see the house and help out, I don't know how to feel about his family still. His sister likes me, I know that, but I don't know if she's just a spy or secret mole that's trying to get information to feed to Cole's dad. And I know that the fact that I'm uncomfortable around his family is because they think so highly of Cole and didn't expect him to have an 'unconventional' relationship. I genuinely think that they were living in a bubble, and I burst it. And Coles sister Michelle has breathed fresh air because of me.

And his mum and dad hate me for it. Michelle is so sweet. I hope she is anyway.

I wobble out of the treatment room, with my dignity *somewhat* intact after getting my labia and arsehole out to someone who's known me for well over ten years. In fact, I was Annas model when she done her intimate wax training when I freshly turned sixteen. I don't think Cole has seen as much of me as Anna has. And she's been waxing me every four weeks since then. My legs already exhausted from the ten-metre walk to the nail bar, my mum *always* does my nails, she always has, even now when she doesn't work hands on in the salon much anymore, she always does my nails. It's one of the reasons we never had any huge arguments, I knew that my nails would be needing infilled soon and wouldn't want anyone else to do it, so I always apologised and made thinks right even when it wasn't my fault.

"So, my love, how are *you* feeling?" She asks as she works her way around my cuticles. She emphasises the word 'you' because as of lately no one cares how I am and just how the baby is. I'm being very dramatic with that. Cole always wants to know how I feel. I'm meaning in general, bumping into people they ask how I am, but their eyes and hands go to the bump. When they see me, they see a pregnant person. Not me. Not Ophelia.

I ponder my answer for a second. Because I feel awful and big and round. But I've also just moved into an amazing house with my fiancé. And my business is going great even though I've had to close my online store because of moving and because of the whole about to pop at any minute thing. I guess I just feel like everything is going too well and everything for once feels normal and I don't know how to handle it.

"Everything is normal. Which is weird." I sigh, feeling the weight on my shoulders lift as soon as I say it. If anyone understands this, it's my mum. She's been through some stuff. And I don't feel like I can talk to Cole about it. I just don't think he'd understand. *His un-traumatic family. Yuck.*

"That's how I felt too. I felt like I didn't deserve it and that something was bound to go wrong. You deserve everything that you have right now Ophelia. I know you don't feel like you do, but you do." Her eyes fall back to my hands while I process what she said. "I know I was an awful role model for you. And I have tried for years to work through everything in my life. But you deserve to have a normal life with a partner and a baby and your dream job. And I know that you think you can only have one or the other, but you can have it all."

She really does know how to give the best pep talks.

"Thanks mum."

As much as I want to tell my mum that she *was* and *is* a good role model there will always be a part of me that hates that she broke herself trying to do good for me. She stayed married to my dad for too long and in that process, she broke, and she took me down with her. And she knows that. My mum isn't a bad mum. She's incredible. But I always felt like, especially in my teen years she was more of a sister than a mum.

I'm going to be a really good mum and be the best role model for my daughter.

Chapter

4

I feel so fresh and free staring down at my French manicured nails and my silky soft (still very swollen) feet, bursting like a ham out of my flip flops, the sole of the flip flops slapping against the soles of my feet. Pulling my trench coat jacket around my body to conceal the bump to stop the stares. I juggle my phone and my keys to find my car keys. I hardly fit behind the wheel but the fifteen-minute drive is fine by me. And I think the drive back home will do me good. I spin around the corner to the car park, staring at the pavement. “Whoa.” I gasp, nearly colliding with a twin buggy.

"Oh my gosh I'm so sorry." My heart skips a beat when I hear that voice. His voice. "Ophelia." He says it so beautifully. The way he always said it. I hear the deep sorrow breath in his voice.

My eyes trail along the beautiful set of twins and my eyes finds his. "Blake." I'm seventeen again and falling in love for the first time. "Hi." I whimper, choking on the lump in my throat. The word 'hi' is all I can seem to muster up the courage to say.

"Hi." Blake sighs. His eyes are still as sad as they were five years ago. Still as full and empty at the same time. "How are you?" He asks swallowing his tears, watching his throat slowly roll.

I don't know what to say. I don't have anything to say. I have so much to tell him, and I can't say any of it. Because everything that I have to tell him is everything I said I didn't want to happen. *Deep breath.* "Well, um... how are you?" I ask the same question he asked me even though I know his answer. Altering my voice as though I'm a cartoon to make me sound animated.

"I'm good... These rascals are Sophie and Jackson... this is daddy's friend Ophelia." He looks at them and points to me. I love how he says my name. I know that he says something about his wife and his job, but I don't listen. Because all I can think about is how much of an incredible dad he is. And how happy I am to see him. I can imagine him rumbling around his house being the universe for his kids.

"Well, um..." I unwrap my arms from around my coat and reveal my bump. Baby girl kicks me when I do as if to announce herself.

"Oh my gosh congratulations." He exclaims. His hair is longer now, like he doesn't have the time to cut it as much anymore. I tuck a lock of hair behind my ear, reminding me how he used to do that. "You're engaged?" His blue eyes bulge when he spots the ring on my finger when I don't hide it. almost making it look like I'm trying to flash it and show it off. When I'm most definitely not.

"Yeah. His name is Cole. I met him just after I moved." I have so much that I want to say to Blake right now. Like how many times I thought about him and how sorry I am and ask him if he thought the same things. But I don't know how to.

We stand in silence for a minute. I just look at him, and he just looks at me. Our eyes wandering across each other. Sophie and Jackson babbling. "Well, I need to go. But it was good seeing you." He shakes himself back into reality. I haven't seen or spoken to Blake in around four years. Yet it feels like no time has passed. But I don't want him to go.

"Right. I'll see you around." I whisper. I start to walk around the buggy, but I find myself in Blake's arms like we're magnetised. My face in his chest. His head leaning on top of mine, taking in his musky, clean smell. I regret our last hug so much; it was full of sadness and hate and anxiety. He kisses my hair like he has done hundreds of times before. I feel his breath quiver when I feel a single tear fall from my eye. "You didn't text me back." I say, my voice muffled by his jacket.

"I wanted to. But if I did, I would have fallen back in love with you all over again." I hate that he says that. Because I know it's true.

"I know." I don't say me too, for a few reasons. I'm pregnant with Cole's child, I'm engaged to Cole. I fall more in love with Cole every single day. And because I don't think I ever fully fell *out* of love with Blake. I will always love him. He is a part of me. He always will be. Blake will forever be my first love. But the main reason I don't say it is because I know I would have too. "I'm glad that you didn't fall back in love with me…in the nicest way possible." I'm glad, because then I would have never become who I am today. I wouldn't be as successful as I am now, because I would have done everything to please him, and would have ended up giving up everything that I am. No matter how good it felt all those years ago to be loved by Blake, it destroyed me. And it felt really good. Air separates us and it feels just as heart-breaking as the last time we parted.

"I'm proud of you Ophelia." He says, smiling at me one last time.

I am too.

"Thank you." I sigh at the sight of him again. "You're a good dad." Patting his arm before I slide around him, not looking back. Because I know that if I look back, I'll break.

I never doubted him for a second, even when we were eighteen. He wanted to be a good dad; he was scared of turning out like his dad. He wanted to be a good dad.

Slamming my driver side door behind me, I don't remember the walk here. I don't remember unlocking my car.

I can't go home right now.

I have spent an hour wandering about home bargains. Wondering what to say to Cole when I get home. Home to my fiancé, home to my new home. Never in a million years would I have thought that I would be where I am today. When I was thirteen, I didn't think I would make it past eighteen, and here I am at twenty-two, contemplating buying a third lamp for my bedroom in my house. I don't think I came in here to buy another lamp or another candle or another throw pillow. I came in here because I didn't want to go home yet. Which is ridiculous because everything and everyone I love is at home.

Seeing Blake today made me relive all those things from all those years ago. What would have happened to me if I stayed with Blake? I don't think I would have been happy. In fact, I know I wouldn't be happy, because even after a five-minute interaction with him, I'm stumbling around a shop filling a trolley with stuff I don't need because I'm too sad to go home to my loving fiancé who's working *tirelessly* to build furniture for our child's bedroom. I think if I were to put it into some form of words, seeing Blake reminds me of all the sad things that have happened to me. And it reminded me of how broken I was when I first met him. And he rebuilt me, until I broke again. And I built myself back up again. And I don't want to break again. I can't. I don't think I could rebuild myself this time.

Chapter

5

“Hi honey, I’m home!” I shout, staggering in the front door, trailing a bag of throw pillows behind me. Dropping the bag in the hallway. The smell of paint has mellowed, and everything seems peaceful, for once. And I’m so fucking glad to be home.

“Hello my love.” Cole shuffles out of the first room in the hall sneakily, closing the door behind him. “You look amazing.” He compliments me. he does that a lot. And every time he does it makes my heart to somersaults. His arms wrap around my shoulders, lifting me up slightly. Taking the weight of the day from me. "How are you feeling?" He asks softly, like the same way you would ask a child.

"I'm okay..." I release his hug. "I ran into someone." *Deep breath.* "I ran into my ex, Blake." I hate that I said his name. Because it just makes me feel seventeen again. It makes me feel broken again. Cole knows how much Blake meant to me and how bad I felt for hurting him.

He takes a second to construct a reply. "Do you want to talk about it?" I hate that Cole is handling this so well. If it was him that ran into his first love and came home and told me, I'm pretty sure I would be freaking out.

I nod.

Coles hand on the small of my back, leading me into the living room, slumping onto the white fluffy couch, that will not stay white nor fluffy by the time that baby girl comes along. Cole sits next to me, an arm around the back of my neck, the other hand on the bump. "Talk to me." He urges, but not sternly or angrily, he says it sweetly and exactly how I want it to be said. He says it exactly how he'll say it to our daughter.

"I ran into him, *literally*... he has two kids, a wife, and everything that he wanted. And I'm really happy for him." I start to tear up now. "And I… have everything I didn't realise I wanted. But when I saw him and spoke to him, I felt seventeen again. I felt broken again and I realised, I don't want our daughter to ever feel like that. And I want our daughter to be sure of herself, confident, be happy and content. I don't want our daughter to feel like I felt when I was seventeen." I don't want my daughter to end up alone in her best friend's bedroom with her knickers at her ankles in pain. And then end up hopeless and broken. My hands jump to my face to wipe my tears. Cole pulls me to his chest, holding me there. Not saying anything. But I really want him to say something right about now.

"What happened to you Ophelia?" He asks, kissing my head. But not asking in a way that he wants to know, more like he's just wondering and feels the need to break the silence. Cole doesn't really know much about my past. I don't like talking about things that happened when I was younger. I haven't felt the need to talk about it, because I haven't thought about it for a long time. I've never had a panic attack while we've had sex, I've never questioned Cole in the slightest, because even after being together for almost four years and having sex probably close to a thousand times he always asks me if I want to and treats me so gingerly and lovingly that he has never once reminded me of when I was raped.

I remember that night so vividly, even though I haven't thought about it for a while. The walls feel like there closing in on me. I'm back in Dans bedroom and I can't breathe. The memories of that night are fuzzy, but I'll never forget the sheer mental pain that I felt, the possessiveness, consuming, animalistic presence that I never want to feel again. Coles not like that. He's loving, affectionate, soft, he's everything that…Brian wasn't. Cole is everything I want, and it took me a long time to realise it. "I was raped. When I was seventeen. And it broke me." I pause wiping the tears dripping down my face. "I met Blake and he helped build me back up. And seeing him today made me sad because it reminded me of how broken I used to be and how I don't want to be broken again. And I'm scared that our daughter will end up broken." I want our daughter to have nothing painful to break her.

Cole's breath deepens and he holds me even closer. "You didn't deserve that, Ophelia." That's the first time anyone has told me that. And he's right. I didn't deserve for all the crappy things that happened to me to happen. He holds my face in his hands, stroking the side of my head.

I stare up at his face, so beautiful, his hair, so golden, his eyes, so bejewelled, his mouth, says perfect things so perfectly. Like he has scripts that he writes and that's how can articulate everything so beautifully.

"I love you." I say as a whisper so no one but us can hear it even though I'm pretty sure it's just us in the house, I probably should have checked before I gave Cole a trauma dump.

"I love you too." kissing my forehead. "But you're going to love me a whole lot more in a second." He grunts as he stands up, pulling me up with him. Steering me back into the hall. Cole knows me better than I know myself. he knows that I block everything out and I'd rather not talk about this for longer than I have to.

"What have you been up to?" I smile, wiping the cuff of my sleeve along my eyes, letting him drag my hand behind him.

"I know that moving has been an emotional rollercoaster for you and you need a constant space that's how you like it to escape. So. May I present... Self Care Co headquarters." He wafts the door open and reveals the room.

So amazing. It's like a mini version of my flat. All my prints on the walls, an entire wall full of shelving, each stocked with my products, and entire section dedicated to my first book 'Loving Me'. Directly under the window I have a desk with drawers on each side, my computer on the desk, complete with a new mousepad.

"I know it's still got some work to go, but." Cole says as I spin round to him leaning on the door.

I rush to him, encasing myself in him. I don't think he realises how much this means to me. I didn't ask him to do this. I don't even think I wanted him to do this. He just did it, because he knew that it would be important to me. He put things up on walls and rearranged the furniture and unpacked some boxes. Not because I'm too pregnant to do it (I am) but because he knew that I wouldn't ask for his help. And that I needed his help. "Thank you." This exactly what I needed after the past few hours.

"You're welcome my love." He kisses the top of my head. "You have fun in here okay. Michelle went to the shop quickly to get us snacks, but she's on unpacking and putting away duty, I'm going to attempt to build the wardrobes. You're only job for the next two weeks until your due date is to keep our daughter safe, fed and happy, and I expect the same for you."

I sit in my spinny desk chair as he taps the doorframe. But before he leaves. "Cole."

He spins back around.

"I haven't thought about what happened to me for a long time. And that's because of you. So, thank you."

It's true. Cole has never made me think about what happened to me. He cut my rapist out of his life, no questions asked, and he didn't even know he was my rapist. I appreciate that Cole didn't make it a 'big thing' which of course it is. But one of the reasons I didn't tell him about it is because I don't want him to look at me and see it.

Cole looks me up and down and starts to speak but then stops himself. "What is it?" I ask.

"I never asked you at the time because you didn't want me to. But I think I know why you wanted him out of my life. Was it Brian?" I remember that day too, storming out of his flat, and how I wish I would have slapped Brian across his smug face. And I would have slapped the ugly out of him, and I would have punched and kicked out all of my anger and frustration that he had caused. And how I would have felt so much better if I had done that. But instead, I was the level-headed, calm and collected Ophelia who balled up all of those feelings and emotions and grouped them together into a speech that would make him question himself. But how I wish I would have slapped him.

I swallow hard, the nightmares come back to me when he says his name. I feel weak, brittle, soft, everything that I don't want to be. Biting my lip to stop me from breaking.

Knock knock

"It's just me, the doors open." I hear Dans voice echo in the semi empty hall. Dan trots into the room. Feeling the tension and sadness that is far too familiar.

I've never seen Cole angry. But I think that is the closest thing I can compare to the look on his face. But he's not angry at me, he would never be angry at me. His face growing red and his scowl growing stronger. I don't like Cole when he's angry.

"I need a minute." Cole says, tensing his jaw and disappearing into the hall.

"Sorry have I walked in on an argument?" Dan whispers, closing the door once Cole escapes.

"I just told Cole about what happened at your party… he used to live with Brian." I can imagine them, sharing pints of milk, arguing over who ate the last of the cereal. "I can't see him like this. Can you make sure he's, okay?" I ask Dan. Me and Dan have never spoke about that night. And we don't intend to.

Dan silently nods before leaving the headquarters and going to find Cole.

I don't like people when they're angry. I don't like *me* when I'm angry. Cole is not an angry man though, he's the man that is wrote about in cheesy romance books that never raise their voice and never slam a door. Cole has never done either of those things. He brings me tea and tucks me into bed when I'm not feeling well. Cole is not an angry man.

The house grows silent when I hear the front door opening. *I need a chain lock on that door.* I want the house to be quiet for a few more minutes. One so I can collect my thoughts and two so I can eery wig on Dan and Cole.

"Hi Ophelia. I've been to the shops for you, I got some stuff to stock your cupboards and fridge." Her organised Ness and need to be perfect make me cringe. The fact that I have lived here for two weeks now and haven't so much as done a big food shop slap me in the face. Michelle bursts in the room, her cheery face drooping when she sees mine. "What's wrong?" She asks, dumping the bags and kneeling down beside me, me still in my spinny chair.

How do I explain? *I don't.*

Ignoring Michelle, I make a bee line to the hall, peeking around the corner, my fingers trailing on the fresh white walls. Squeezing past the boxes that still aren't unpacked.

Cole is sitting at the kitchen island, head in his hands. "I mean how did that happen to her?" Coles hands wipe the tears running down his cheeks. He's not angry. He's sad. Sad that someone could hurt me.

"It's not my business to tell you Cole. But trust me, he will never touch anyone ever again. And if Lia didn't tell you about it, she had her reasons." Dan eyes me, ushering me over with his eyes.

I'm confused by what Dan said. 'He will never touch anyone ever again.' I puzzle my eyes at him. "What do you mean Dan?"

"Let's just say. My mums a lawyer. And she can cover some things up." I dismiss what Dan says because I'm no longer interested in his words right now. Coles arms wrap around me and bump, his head resting on my shelf of a tummy. I tilt my head directing Dan out of the kitchen. I can hear the office door close and the muffled sound of

Michelle's voice still confused as to what's going on.

Deep breath. I try and construct a statement in my head. "I've been through a lot of stuff Cole. And I haven't told you about a lot of it. And I have my reasons for it. I don't want everything that's happened to me to determine how you treat me. The version of myself that went through stuff is not the same Ophelia that you know. I left that version of myself in a box at a fire station a long time ago." I try to laugh it off, because in these situations you can either be sad, or laugh. I like to imagine it sometimes, packing up seventeen-year-old me, putting a blanket and a water bottle in the box beside her, kissing her head and telling her that it'll be alright. I hope she found her way.

Coles head tilts up to meet me as I balance myself on another bar stool. Stroking my face with his teary hands, my heart melts when he twiddles my earrings with his fingers, admiring every diamante. "I want to fall in love with every version of you Ophelia. the good, the bad and everything in between."

I don't know how he can do that when I can't.

Chapter 6

I remember the night my mum and dad broke up as if it was last night. I was in my bedroom crying. Because I was so sick and tired of my dad being angry at my mum. Being jealous, being awful. My mum had just finished a twelve-hour shift at the salon, I was getting ready for bed when I heard her come in, I smiled, ready to rush down the stairs and give her a hug before I tucked myself into bed. Still with toothpaste on my chin and toothbrush in my mouth I peeked over the banister. I was wearing white pyjamas with unicorns on them, and the unicorns had a pink and purple mane, and the horn was silver and glittery and there were probably various stains on them, but they were my favourite. I waved at her even though she couldn't see me. She didn't even have her bag off of her shoulder when my dad shouted. "Where have you been?" He scowled it so nastily. My mum looked up to the banister to make sure I wasn't there; I was she just didn't see me. I got good at hiding. "Voice down Charlie." She whispered. "I told you I was working a late night tonight." Her voice was quiet, volume wise, but her voice didn't have the same strength and panache behind it as I remember it now. She didn't sound like herself. Like she was quietened. I didn't like hearing my mum not being her confident and proud self. I peered over the banister, wiping the toothpaste from my chin, watching her finally put her handbag down and walk into the kitchen. Her hair was still exactly how it was when she dropped me off at my grans house that morning, it had snowed, and I couldn't find my gloves, so she didn't want me getting my hands cold on the walk. The bouncy blow-dry still somehow perfect after working all day. "I'd just appreciate it if you didn't spend all day at work." Dad's voice scowled as mum put a plate in the microwave. I could hear the tears curl up in my mum's voice. "Charlie. Please don't speak to me like that." She was tired, all she wanted to do was go home and not be belittled.

That's when I ran into my room. Because I couldn't stand the fact that mum was upset, and it was my dad that was making her upset. I leaped under my covers and started crying, muffling my tears with my blanket, because I was scared that my dad would see me upset and speak to me like he spoke to mum. And even at eight I knew that I deserved better than to be spoken to like that.

"Ophelia. are you okay?" My mums sweet, beautiful voice is back, her cold body leaning over me, sitting on my bed, pulling the covers off of my head. "I'm sorry you heard that." That wasn't the worst argument or thing I heard or seen. But I hated every second of it just the same. I hated seeing a bad side to someone I was supposed to love and cherish.

"I don't like the way he speaks to you. And I don't want to hear him like that again mum." I said through my tears. My mum stroking my hair.

"You won't need to ever again Ophelia. I'm sorry. I love you." My mums necklace hit the back of my head as she lay down beside me, still with her coat and shoes on. Her stomach most likely still empty. Her perfume filled the air as I fell asleep. The faint sound of the microwave beeping.

I woke up the next morning and she wasn't beside me. I felt for her in the covers when my eyes were still shut. I crept out of my room, scared for what argument might be unleashing below. But everything was silent and somehow peaceful.

My mum's bedroom door opened as she floated out of it, as if she'd just had the best sleep of her life. She knelt down and hugged me tight, her bouncy blow-dry still perfect from the morning before, her pyjamas smelling like her perfume. "This is mine and your house now. No one else. I'm sorry I let dad speak to me like that. Don't let anyone ever speak to you like that." Her eyes were red like she had been crying all night, but there was relief behind it.

It was a Sunday morning. We spent the day decorating the house for Christmas. I came across one of those personalised ornaments with a mum, dad and a child, each with our names under them. I remember holding it in my hands, close to my heart and realising that it would never be on the tree again. We baked cookies and spent the night watching movies and for the first time ever I looked at my mum and she looked genuinely happy. She was fixed.

Cole's face gets sadder and sadder the more I look at it. "So that's why Christmas is hard?" He asks. I nod. Cole's hand finds bump. "She's never going to hate Christmas okay." His voice is more delicious than ever. "I love you." He says leaning into me.

"I love you too." His hands find my face and his lips find mine. His lips are more delicious than ever too. His body leaning over me ever so gingerly, scared to make a movement that will make me feel like how I did when I was seventeen. It's midnight. And I've spent the past six hours pouring my heart and soul out to Cole. And we've cried our entire way through it. Telling him about every single emotion I've had and every bad thing that's happened to me. Every interaction with a bully, every fake friendship I had, every time I had a puddle shower when I held my face under the water to feel relief. I even told him about my diary, I haven't written in it for a long time, because I don't feel like I need to anymore. But I told him about all of the feelings that I wrote down and all the times I cried into it treating it like my friend. "You don't need to treat me like a house of cards Cole." I part our kiss, even though I want to kiss him still. "I'm not scared of you. I've never feared you. I've always known that no matter what happened between us you would treat me exactly how I wanted to be treated." I comb my fingers through his golden locks, pushing them out of his perfect face.

"I always treated you how you deserve to be treated. Like the perfect princess you are." Both of his hands work their way to the back of my neck, playing with the stray hairs that are too short for my ponytail. "I love every part of you Ophelia." He admits.

I grin, pulling his face to mine, smooshing our lips together and I feel the same fireworks that I felt during our first kiss all those years ago, the fireworks that I feel every time we kiss, every time he looks at me. I feel the exact same way that I felt that day in the coffee shop. The only difference is that I've fallen even more madly in love with him every day. And I used to think that that would be a scary thing. It's not so scary anymore. Especially right now when he carries me up to bed and makes love to me even more lovingly than he ever has before.

Chapter 7

Cole comes back into the bedroom, his boxers on backwards. He carries a plate of cheese and crackers in one hand and a tub of chocolate ice cream in the other. My two favourite pregnancy cravings. He tosses me over the throw blanket that the floor swallowed to cover me up with. Because I don't have the effort to put my clothes back on. "Here you go princess." He flops himself into bed next to me, propping up the pillows so I can sit up. Kissing my head when he does.

"Thank you." I say, taking a bite of a cracker, looking over at Cole as he takes one himself.

“You don’t need to say thank you my love.” He laughs.

“Oh not for the crackers, for the sex, that was really good.” I say sarcastically. I aint lying though. It was *really* good.

He almost chokes on a cracker when I say that. “It was really good.” He laughs again agreeing with me, nodding his head ferociously.

I take the television remote from the bedside table and try and settle on a movie, then I go back to the old favourite tv show ‘friends.’ “I feel bad referring our daughter as bump. We need to think of a name, cause I’m about to pop any minute.” I never put any thought into picking out a name until now. A lot of young women have lists on their phones of possible baby names, but I never thought I’d settle down and have one, so I didn’t bother to make a list.

“Don’t tell me you don’t have a list on your phone?” Cole jumps up, almost knocking the cheese off the plate. “I have a list!” He exclaims.

Of course Cole would have a fucking list. Just another way his happy, healthy (ish) family has served him well.

“I want a name that matches mine as selfish as that sounds.” I blurt out. I’ve always loved my name, even though all through school there would be someone who couldn't pronounce it, or coffee shops can never spell it right, it felt good knowing that my name was unique. "Something flowery and feminine." The chocolate ice cream gets torn open, Cole hands me a spoon. His arm behind my head now, his hand trailing along my bare shoulder.

"What about her last name?" He asks, licking his spoon clean.

And I'm a child again. I have my mums last name, I always have and I'm proud to have her last name, but it was the cause of many arguments. It made my dad feel like an outsider. I dump the spoon back into the tub. Imagining the awkward arguments and conversations I would overhear. People assumed that my dad was my step-dad, especially because I'm also the spitting image of my mum, my mum never wanted me to have his name, because she didn't want his name. They were in love for many years, but she just didn't want people to know her as 'Charlie's wife' she wanted to be Cherry Bloom. Her name is straight from a poem, I can imagine the poem being written beneath a cherry blossom tree, written in a leather journal by a woman with long frizzy hair and crystal jewellery. That's why my mum wanted to keep her name, and for me to have it. My mums mum didn't keep her own name and after her parents got divorced, her mum kept her married name to please others. My mum would never do such a thing. She didn't discuss it with my dad because she already knew that would never change her mind. So, there I was- Ophelia Opal Bloom. The cause of many arguments where my dad felt emasculated and small. Sort of how he made my mum feel in the long run.

"I want her to have yours."

"I want her to have yours."

We both say it in unison.

"Oh, come on Beckford is such a stupid last name!" Cole laughs. "My parents didn't even think twice about my name. I love your name, the whole thing." He says as I smile, facing the tub of partially melted ice cream.

"Beckford hyphen Bloom." I suggest, but not really suggesting, because I can tell by the way that Cole is looking at me, he already agrees.

"This is why I love you, Ophelia." He leans over to me, stealing a kiss. Looking at me with those stupidly perfect eyes of his, glancing them up and down my face unapologetically when he pulls away from our kiss. "And I want her to have your name as a middle name." He says, brushing his thumb over my lip.

Jesus Christ this child's name is going to be a mouthful. "I think it might be considered child abuse to have that many syllables in a name." I giggle.

"How about just Lia?" His smile grows when he says it. "I hope she's just like you." Whispering softly, his hand still on my lips.

"You'll have your work cut out for you then." I fire back sarcastically. Cole rolls his eyes, grabbing my face and pushing his lips to mine again. I let out another laugh, throwing myself back, pulling him on top of me. He tosses the blanket covering my boobs to the side and kisses every part of me.

Chapter

8

One part of pregnancy that will forever confuse me is the insomnia. Even when I do sleep I wake up even more tired. I've been lying on my side trying to fall asleep for almost two hours now. Cole is lying flush with me, one arm under my head and the other pulling me closer to him and periodically brushing it over baby girl, Lia, Beckford-Bloom. It makes me feel good that he loves me so much. *Obviously.* But I never thought that I would actually happen. The fact that someone loves me enough to want to be with me forever, have a child with me. I never thought I wanted that with anyone. I guess it sometimes just takes one person to realise that that's what you want. It just takes one person to realise that you deserve what you've been holding yourself back from. A happy family. I can just imagine us in a few months' time, in this exact position only with a bundle of joy, and she'll be playing with our fingers and making cute baby noises. And I'll have the family that I didn't know I deserved.

Owwww

Okay I felt that. The sharp band that feels like lightening striking me.

Owww. Ahh. Okay baby girl. *Take a chill pill.*

I sit up now. Cole is too deep a sleep to notice I've got up. Taking a gulp from the glass of old water on the bedside table. Bending over to collect my clothes from the floor. Pain strikes along my lower back, sending a gasp out my mouth. I have two weeks left. But something tells me that she doesn't want to be in here any longer. But I don't want her to leave. She keeps me safe because I keep her safe. Because of her I do all the stupid things adults are supposed to do. I eat five fruits and veg a day. I take vitamins, I rest, I go on a walk every day. And I feel so good about doing all those things. Because it's for her. It's all for her.

Pulling on my t-shirt, I get out of bed. Cole still hasn't moved a muscle.

I haven't spent much time in her bedroom yet. I trace my hand along the wall to steady myself through each bout of pain, flipping on the light switch in her bedroom. The room isn't fully finished yet, it's painted white and the cot and drawers are built, but I still have a pile of decorations that I want to put up but never found the right moment. *I guess there's no time like the present.*

Wafting through the pile of clean clothes, finding the perfect place for everything. I've organised all of her baby grows into one drawer, vests in another, an entire drawer dedicated to teeny tiny baby socks. I think there's a whole massive stereotype of new mums, where they spend days at a time organising all of the new babies' stuff and that's all they ever want to talk about. I don't feel that way. At all. Like yes obviously I'm excited to meet her and spend time with her, but I'm not orgasming over a new bottle steriliser.

What's the rhyme? Five-one-one babies going to come? Five contractions, each lasting a minute for one hour. I think I've got that beat. I check the time on my phone. Four forty-six. Great, she's a morning person.

Staggering back into mine and Cole's bedroom. "Cole." I shake his shoulder, leaning over him, still in the same position I left him in over an hour ago.

"Mhmh." He sighs. His eyes slowly fluttering open.

"It's time." I don't realise it, but I'm smiling.

Chapter

9

"You are going to be an amazing mum." Cole says, gripping my leg with one arm, his other arm behind my neck, holding me up into some sort of weird, rejected pretzel. You know the ones that they give out as free samples in shopping centres. That's what I look like right now.

I don't have the energy right now to reply to him and say 'but I don't know if I will be.' I am going to love and adore her but I'm not going to be one of those mums that goes to every school play, I'm not going to go to all the parents' meetings. I won't be a picture-perfect mum. But I *will* be the one that orders a Chinese when she's sad. I will hold her on my lap when she cries. I'll always be on her team. But I'm scared that I won't be good enough.

I'm pushing and I can feel everything but nothing at the same time. I can't quite make out what my midwife is saying to me. Everything is a blur and I'm in my own head. Everything is in slow motion, but also going too fast. I feel amazing. I feel like an actual machine. "You are incredible." I can hear Cole say.

Breathe.

"Congratulations mum." I feel like I've just woke up from a fever dream. Or this is a fever dream. I'm not too sure.

That's when I hear the cry.

That glorious cry.

I'm happy.

My smile gleaming up at the ceiling, not sure for who I'm thanking right now. But I'm thankful for someone.

"You have done so good baby." Coles lips squish to mine.

Him. Cole. That's who I'm thankful for.

Wrapped up in a towel, a perfect ball of perfection lands on my chest. I glance down at her as her eyes look up at me. Her perfect green, brown eyes staring back at me. I feel like I'm in a time machine and I'm looking at myself. And she's perfect.

"I love you so much." Coles arms wrap around us. His tears trickling down his face. I feel like I'm consumed. And not in a bad way that I always thought it would be. In the best way possible I feel consumed, protected, loved.

"Thank you. Thank you. Thank you." I keep repeating myself. The tears streaming down my face now.

Cole releases me, holding my face in his hands. "What for?" He asks.

"For loving me when I thought I couldn't be."

My answer sends us into floods of tears and suddenly it's just us. Everything goes quiet. And it's me, Cole, baby girl and the love that we share. I think of all the times I would lie in bed at night when I was younger. I never knew a love like this existed. I longed for the love that I watched in movies and read about in books or listened to in songs, but I didn't think it existed. Until now.

Chapter 10

"Flora Lia Beckford-Bloom." Cole smiles down at me when I say it.

"Beautiful. Just like her mum." I reach my lips up to his. My arms are cramped up from holding her, but I don't want to let her go. I miss her. And she's right here. But I miss having her closer to me. "I'm proud of you Ophelia." Proud of me for what? I don't know. But I'm not questioning it. Because I like how it makes me feel when he says it.

I was very strict when I told everyone that I didn't want visitors when I was in hospital. I want these next few weeks to be ours. Cole has six weeks off of work, I'm going to try and take as much time away from Self Care Co as possible, but I'll still be running my social medias. And once I get into a proper routine I want to work on my second book more seriously. I want to have everything together and feel more like myself before I have anyone round to the house. I hate seeing new mums and dads exhausted from looking after their new baby and then as soon as they get a minute to themselves the doorbell goes and half your bloody family comes rushing in and you need to make them a cup of tea. *Fuck that.* Door is getting locked, and we can be hermits until we feel ready.

I haven't said much in the past few hours since Flora has been born. I think there's too much to say and not a good enough way to say it. It all just feels too surreal.

"I love you." I whisper to Cole as he carefully places her in her crib.

"I love you too mama." Creeping over to me quietly, kissing my head. My hair in an extremely messy ponytail. I've been a mum for four hours now. Cole clambers onto the bed beside me, resuming our snuggling position from before my bump got too big. My head on his chest and his right arm holding my hand.

When I found out I was having a girl I tried to hide my fear. I think I've done a good job of it so far. But I'd be lying if I said I wasn't absolutely terrified. I'm petrified. For her to grow up. Grow up and become a statistic.

The first time I was cat called I was thirteen. I was in my school uniform. My hair was in pleats. I looked like and was a child. I remember back then, being terrified every time I walked to or from school because chances are I would have had a car honk, a sleezy statement shouted at me, or the worst of all was the stares. Because you didn't know what they were thinking. What they we're fantasising about. I worried for the women in their lives. Did they have a wife, a daughter, a sister? Did they think that about them? Were they safe?

For years I told everyone that my favourite colour was blue even though it was pink. All because I hated the comment 'pink to make the boys wink'. As a seven-year-old I couldn't understand why I would go out of my way to wear something to please boys. I'm scared my daughter will feel that way. 'Be unapologetically feminine.' That's what I will tell her. Or don't be. Never apologise for how you dress, act or speak.

My daughter is going to be absolutely incredible. I'll make sure of it. She will have manners but be a smart ass when she needs to be, and she won't apologise for it. I want to be *her* when I grow up.

I want to be a good mum. I want to be the person I wish I had growing up.

Chapter 11

Today is the day that we get to go home. All three of us. My family.

I've been cooped up in this hospital room for one day too many. I stink. I haven't been able to have a proper wash. My vagina feels and probably looks like I've had a failed vaginal reconstruction. I don't even want to look down there after seeing Flora and knowing that she came out of there.

Cole has packed up all of our stuff in my mini suitcase. I heavily underestimated the amount of stuff I would need to bring for myself. I've decided to bottle feed, but my boobs didn't quite catch the memo, so I've went through way too many tops because my nipples keep bursting out drops of milk. The first stop when we get out of here is the supermarket so I can get cabbage to put on my boobs. Old wives' tales always seem to do the trick.

A scarily slow drive and a trip to the supermarket later, Cole is pulling into the driveway at a snail's pace. I'm sitting in the back seat, overseeing and examining every movement, noise and breath coming from Flora. I heard horror stories of babies in car seats, and it makes me never want to have her in a car again.

My vagina throbbing in the *least* sexy way possible I waddle myself out of the car and into the house. The house that I forgot was a complete bomb site. *Fuck.*

Cole comes in behind me, his arms full, Flora in her car seat in one hand and my suitcase in the other. "It's okay. Leave it to me darling." He says, sensing my distaste for the clutter and the smell of stale rubbish. *We definitely should have asked for someone to come in and have a wipe round for us.* "This is your time." He says assertively. Placing the car seat onto the couch. "You've spent eight and a half months literally building a human. And you've just had it fire out of you. You deserve to relax. I will worry about the rest." He takes my hands, leaning me down onto the couch. "I love you." Still holding my hands.

"I love you too." I whisper, holding back my smile. But holding back tears at the same time.

I'm sitting on the couch. I took Flora out of her terrifying bomb of a car seat, and I have her in my arms. Which now that I think of it, seem less safe. I don't know what to do. There's not a nurse, or a midwife here to help. I'm lost. I start breathing faster and my breaths keep getting shorter. I'm looking down at my sleeping baby and I don't know what to do. Cole comes into the living room, noticing that I haven't even taken my shoes off yet and we've been home for half an hour now. "Are you okay?" He asks, going onto his knees and loosening my shoes for me, sliding one shoe off at a time. "It's going to be okay Ophelia." He's sitting next to me now, taking Flora from my arms.

Deep breath.

Closing my eyes and letting my body feel the air filling my lungs.

"Do you want to go for a shower sweetheart. I've got this." He kisses my shoulder. I nod. "I'll go get it ready for you." He kisses my shoulder again. Speaking to me as he does.

How is Cole so good at this. He has somehow, unpacked, cleaned up and is taking care of me. When all I've done is sit on the couch. I feel lost. Misplaced. Dare I say it. Broken. Not broken. Definitely not broken. I can't be broken.

I'm still sitting on the couch.

Stuck.

Cole comes back in. "Come on my love. I've got you." He takes my hand and pulls me up, still holding Flora in his other hand. Dragging me up the stairs and into our bathroom. "Do you want help?" He asks ever so gently, not wanting me to be embarrassed.

"No, I'll be okay." I say to him before he slowly walks out, closing the door behind him. I know I won't be. I look into the mirror opposite the shower. My hair greasy and frizzy, my skin dull and lifeless. Slowly stripping the layers of clothes. Tugging the scrunchie out of my hair. The frozen aloe vera adult nappy is the last to go. I stand naked. My stomach still protruding and swollen. My stretch marks saggy and my boobs up to my chin in the worse way possible. Cole already turned on the shower so it's nice and warm and the sound mutes my feelings.

Stepping in and feeling the hot water melt into my skin, feeling my soaked hair cascade down my back, the drops of water trinkling down my legs. I let the water fall onto my face. I start crying. Uncontrollably. And I don't know why. If I could right now, I'd be lying down having a puddle shower.

Every fear I've ever had of being a mother wash over me. The feeling of dread that my daughter will grow up to hate me. That Cole will be tired of me. That I'll never feel like Ophelia again.

The water beating onto my back as I scrub my body with coconut scented deliciousness to distract myself from the burning tears in my eyes.

Knock knock

"I'm just checking on you." Cole says, peering his head in the door. Rushing in when he hears my tears. Grabbing the warm towel from the rail, sliding the shower open and turning off the water. "It's okay, I'm here." He shushes, pulling the towel around me and holding me to his chest, my soaked naked body getting his clothes wet. But he doesn't care. "Let me take care of you." He directs me out of the shower, wrapping me up in the towel. Sliding my slippers in front of my feet and I instinctively put them on.

I don't remember getting into my pyjamas or getting into bed. But I open my eyes and the bedside table is full of 'amenities' a cup of tea, still with steam coming from it, with a side of tea biscuits and a spoon on the side in case I drop any biscuits in. The house seems silent. Like no one is home. But I know that's not true. The sun is shining through the blinds and if I would guess it's four pm. My phone is perfectly placed beside the cup of tea. Yes, it is four. I don't have the energy to get out of this bed, I feel like I've been hit by a truck. One of those huge ones as well that have logs on the back of them that struggle to go up steep hills.

Me- Hi xx

The three dots line the screen for a few seconds.

Cole- Hi, do you want me to come up? X

Me- Yes please xx

I sit up properly in the bed with my back against the headboard, my damp hair getting pulled into an even messier bun than it was a few hours ago. I hear Cole stepping up the stairs.

“Hey mama.” Peering into the room. His face brightens it. Swinging the door open, he looks dishevelled, worn, and still somehow perfect. Baby Flora in his arms sleeping. He sits down on his side of the bed, swinging his legs over so he’s in the same position as me. “Do you want to talk about how you feel?” He asks, taking his hand and pulling tangled hairs back from my dry face.

I sigh. “I just don’t feel like myself. And like we have a baby now and hormones make me crazy.” I try to laugh. But the tears sneak through, wiping my face with the arm of my pyjamas.

Cole puts his free arm around me. “I know it’s crazy. But she’s a pretty cool baby.” He jokes. “But I am here for you. Anytime you need me, okay. You can be as crazy as you want, and you can spend weeks in bed if you want. Because I love you. We love you.”

My eyes fall to Flora. She is perfect. Her white baby grow too big for her and it wrinkles up at her teeny arms. Her pink hat covering most of her hair. She looks how I looked when I was a baby. I want to protect her. I want her to be safe. I want her to be happy. “She looks like you.” Cole declares, kissing my head. “Do you want to come downstairs. And I can order some food for early dinner?”

"Yeah. That would be nice." I utter. I haven't had a proper meal in days.

"Okay take your time." Kissing my head one last time before he gets off the bed and leaves the room, taking Flora with him.

Deep breath

You can do this Ophelia.

One foot at a time, swinging myself onto the side of the bed. Sliding my feet into my slippers.

1

2

3

On my feet, I'm standing.

I did it.

Standing looking out the window. Peering into the neighbours' gardens, rows of washings on lines filled with clothes, an older couple sitting in their back garden on their rocking chairs, they are both reading and sharing a pitcher of what looks like homemade lemonade, but I know that it's probably spiked with alcohol. I wonder if me and Cole will be like that. Grow old together, retired, sit in our garden all day reading books and exchanging memories. I hope we do.

The ounce of hope pushes me into the bathroom. I don't dare look in the mirror. A fresh nappy and a swirl of mouthwash does the trick to wash the sour taste from my mouth.

I stand at the top of the stairs, looking down at the mountain. Wondering how it would feel if I slithered down. What would take the least amount of energy? Walking, sliding down the banister or going down on my arse, that last one might rip my vagina off so walking will do.

One step at a time.

You can do this.

Chapter 12

I'm in a lot of pain. Physically, yes. But also, mentally. I've been able to block out some of my negative thoughts by drinking a god-awful amount of tea and regular snuggles. Flora is a week old now. I've spent most of this week sitting on frozen aloe vera pads. Cole has been amazing. He has taken charge of the nappy changes and the night feeds. I'm in a slump. And I'm aware that I'm in a slump which I would argue is even worse. At least if I didn't know, I wouldn't be aware of it and wouldn't be upset with myself for being in one. But I just can't find the motivation to do anything about it. I feel as though I've done nothing. I know I need to rest and let my body readjust but I still feel like I'm not doing anything worthwhile. Cole has done the majority of the work, and I've hardly made it off this couch.

"I just got her down." Cole whispers, creeping into the living room. Planting as kiss on my head once he reaches me. "How are you feeling?" Coles toxic trait is that he is always perky. *Unbearably perky.* He has had maybe five hours of sleep over the past three days, has been sick on, pooed on, peed on. How is he so God damn perfect?

I shake my head, biting my lip instead of crying.

I don't know how mums do this. The feeling of accomplishing something so massive like building an actual human being inside of you, then pushing that out of you or going through major surgery. But then a few days later feeling like shit. I should be ecstatic. I should be drooling over my new baby and floating on a cloud of baby spew and BO. But I just don't. I don't have the motivation to get off this couch.

"What can I do?" Cole asks. His arm under my head, his body half on the couch.

"Would you hate me if I done some work right now?" I just need to focus on something. I'm overwhelmed by the number of congratulations messages I'm receiving. I need to just be Ophelia for a few hours. And not the mum Ophelia.

"Would you hate me if I *helped* you do some work?"

My body eases and as smile spreads over both our faces.

Waddling into my office, Cole sits the baby monitor on my desk that connects to the one in the dining room where Flora is sleeping soundly. I sent out an email, social media blasts and plastered it all over my website that shipping will be delayed for the next few months until I got everything organised and got me and Flora into a routine. But I need my sanity right now. And if that means packaging up fun stationary and replying to customer emails, I am happy to do that.

My printer is working overtime printing out a weeks' worth of packing slips and shipping labels. "You are still recovering Ophelia. So you are sitting on that chair and you can make sure I'm doing everything right." Cole demands, reaching up to the top shelf and gathering overstock. He looks really good when he does that.

"Understood." I grin. "This is really hard for me, you know that don't you?"

The cardboard box slaps against the floor. "Of course, I do. You're a work acholic." He takes the scissors and slices open the box.

"Yes. But it's also hard for me to see you being everything I ever wanted. And you look really sexy when you do it." I spin around from my computer, biting down on my lip.

I love seeing how amazing Cole is. With Flora and with me. "You look sexy too mama." He strolls over to me, spinning my chair back round to face the computer, his hands trailing up my sides, following the curve of my waist until they're in my hair. His supple lips planting peppered kisses up my neck. My eyes closing and my head tilting back. I open my eyes and his face is above mine. Cole places another kiss on my lips. "I love you my darling." His eyes glare at all of my features. My greasy hair, my pale face, my forehead with hormonal acne dotted around it. "She has your eyes." He whispers.

"I wish she had yours." I say, still with my head tilting up at him.

"Those are the eyes that I fell in love with." His thumb grazing the orbit of my eye, still staring down at me. "I look at her and I fall in love with you all over again."

My heart melts.

Cole has my heart.

My whole heart.

And he can do whatever he wants with it.

But I know that Cole just wants to protect it.

I trust Cole to have my heart. He won't break it. He will nurture it and adore it.

Right on cue, Flora starts crying over the baby monitor. She's not a really cryie baby. She cries when she's hungry, tired or needs changed or most likely when she wants to hear her own voice. "I'll get her my love." Cole bends down and kisses my head.

One thing I've heard a lot in new parent families is that you're often scared that your partner loves your new baby more than you. And while I understand that that's a scary thing to think about. That's how it should be. Because no matter what happens she is the priority. Flora's happiness and safety come first. But oh, how I love how much Cole loves me. And the fact that he loves Flora more makes me love him even more.

"Hi mama. Can I come to work with you?" Cole tip toes in, holding Flora facing out towards me, holding one of her hands up and waving it gently.

Holding out my hands like a crab to reach her. Still sitting in my chair Cole places her on my chest, the weight of her teeny tiny frame makes me smile. Her hair still smelling like that new baby smell. You know that smell that makes your ovaries do somersaults. The cutest little gurgles coming out of her mouth every few minutes that distract me from my work.

It has taken me twelve whole minutes to write this email.

Still carrying her, I slip out of my office, leaving Cole packing up orders. Finding the *way* too fancy baby carrier that wraps around your body that someone bought for me. I got given so much stuff and I don't know where the hell I'm putting it all. Even though we said we wanted peace it didn't stop people sending parcels to our door.

Strutting back into the office, hands like superwoman on my waist. Cole smiles at me when he notices how happy it makes me.

It is take your daughter to work day.

I remember when my mum would take me to work. Usually after school when she couldn't get away early or my gran couldn't look after me. But I would sit in the staff room and read and do homework. Until I got bored anyway. Then I would venture out to the nail bar area. I made up lives for people. And would eery wig on everyone. There was this one lady. She was *easily* sixty. She would come in like clockwork, every two weeks at four o'clock on a Wednesday. She would get bright red nails. She always wore fur coats, even in the summer, she always had fabulous pearl necklaces on. I would get her a cup of tea and she would always give me a pound. She parked right outside the salon, risking getting a parking ticket, her car was yellow and had a pink steering wheel. She was the most fabulous and luxurious woman I had ever met. I never asked her questions. But I asked my mum once I had gotten a bit older what her story was. According to her, she had married her husband, who was properly filthy rich. Which wasn't how the lady worded it, but I think I prefer my mums. She caught him cheating on her. He was very high up in politics I think and had a few sketchy things here and there that couldn't get out. So, she took all his money in exchange for silence. He died from an accidental overdose a year later and she inherited his fortune. She now lives in Edinburgh in an apartment with her friend. She still makes the two hour journey every two weeks to get her nails done.

The baddest bitch of all time.

I loved going to my mum's work. It made me learn how to speak to people. It taught me that everyone has their own problems. Everyone has something they don't want to tell anyone.

Chapter

13

Me- Are you ready to meet your niece uncle Dan? x

Dan- Oh my gosh. Hell yes. X

It's been eight days since Flora has been born. And its been eight days since I've been a mum, and its been eight days of getting to know myself again. My mum came round this morning and dropped off premade dinners and snacks, homemade macaroni and chicken soup. She done the dishes and wiped round the house while she let us sleep on the couch. *She knows the drill.* She is absolutely engrossed with her. Although she says she's not anywhere near old enough to be a gran. Cole's mum is coming over tonight. Which is terrifying. Because I'm certain she doesn't like me. I don't think she even likes Cole now at this point. They haven't spoke much.

"Uncle Dan is here."

"And aunt Lacy."

They clump into the living room, pink balloons and gift bag in hand. Flora is sitting in her bouncer chair fast asleep. "Well done my darling." Lacy says, leaning over the back of the couch to hug me. Tearing up as she does. Sniffing away any evidence of emotion.

"How are you a mum?" Dan asks comically, slithering himself onto the couch next to me, slapping his hand on his head in disbelief almost cartoon like.

"I have no clue how the hell that happened." I laugh. Cole strolls into the living room and Lacy and Dan congratulate him too. Giving him a pat on the back.

"I should probably admit. I've never held a baby before." Dan holds up his hand.

"I seriously question you so much Dan." Lacy sighs.

I chuckle. Because up until Flora I hadn't held a baby for, I don't know how long. I don't think I had ever. Lacy sits down on the floor in front of Flora, trying not to make a sound but at the same time being as noisy as possible to ensure she wakes up.

"I'm going to get her bottle sorted. Dan come through and get yourself and Lacy a drink." He follows behind me. Flora isn't due a bottle for another half an hour, but I need to speak to Dan. I didn't have the chance to ask him, but what did he mean when he told Cole that his mum can 'cover up things'?

Making sure that no one else is following us I fold over my arms and lean against the kitchen worktop. "Sit." I demand. Dan pulls out one of the bar stools with a confused look on his face. "What did you do after that night." I don't need to emphasise or be more detailed. Because he knows exactly what 'that night' means.

"Ahh. It's better for you not to know." Dan tries to slide off of the stool and escape my interrogation.

"Dan." I say sternly. I'm impressed with myself, who is this?

He rolls his head back. "Lia you're like a sister to me. and I'm like your brother. So... I done what any brother would do." I stare at his scrawny frame in confusion. "The next day. After I knew you were safe. I found him. He was at the training grounds at his school. He was waiting on his dad to pick him up. He was the only one there. So, I beat the shit out of him. And he didn't fight back." Dan takes a deep breath once he sees the scene play out in my head. "I wanted to protect you and I didn't know how to because I had already let him in my house." Brian was built. Like he was properly built. He played rugby. He was stronger than me anyway. And a hell of a lot stronger than Dan. "He let me hit him." I bite the inside of my lip. I can't imagine Dan being so vigilant and protective like that. *Yes,* he's like my big brother, but the kind of brother that flirts with your friends and makes jokes, the kind that helps you sneak back into the house if you've been out all night. The kind of brother I'd love Flora to have. "His dad showed up and phoned the police. So, I phoned my mum. And she's a damned good lawyer." I can just imagine Stacy, strutting into the rugby pitch in her skirt and blazer with her high heels slowly sinking into the mud.

I let the picture in my head play out. How good it would have been to see. Brian. Big burly, built like a brick shit hoose, melting into the grass, his face slowly trickling blood. Him accepting defeat. Because he knows what he done was wrong. The satisfaction would have been delicious. To see that look on his face. Similar to the one on mine that night. Defeat. Because that's how I felt that night. Defeated.

"Thank you."

Dan nods, not saying you're welcome because I don't think he wanted a 'thank you'. He kept the secret for years. He didn't want to tell me.

Oh, how I wish I was there.

I have a quick waddle around the house, making sure there isn't a pillow that isn't fluffed or a blanket untucked. There is something about a mother and their son. It's a weird relationship. I have a theory that all mothers of boys secretly want to marry them. Not because they are attracted to them or anything. They just think they can do no wrong, and then shelter them to make them believe their partner isn't good enough. Again, that's another thing I witnessed in the salon. Mother-in-laws from hell were the top topic in the salon. From making weddings about themselves or blatantly being rude to their daughter-in-law, mother-in-law drama was top tier drama.

"Hi mum." Cole swings the front door open as I walk down the hall to reach them. "It's so good to see you." He says before pulling her in for a hug.

I smile awkwardly waiting for her to hug me. But she doesn't, she walks into the living room and completely ignores me. My jaw literally drops. Like good job I'm not drinking anything, or I would need to get the mop out. Cole passes by me. "Don't worry. I've got this." He assures me. I hover in the hall for a few more seconds. Trying to think of reasons she ignored me.

1. She didn't see me. (I was standing pretty much in front of her so that's out the window.)
2. She did say hi, I just didn't hear her. (Cole looked just as shocked as me)
3. I have her precious little boy and have strayed him away from the life she wants him to lead. (Pretty spot on I think)

Peering into the living room. Elizabeth sitting straight up on the couch, examining the room for signs of life and for coats of dusk on my nik naks. She still hasn't said hello to me. I *would* offer her a drink, but I'm feeling *far* too petty for that. "Mum, help yourself to a drink in the kitchen." Cole presents his hands, leading her towards the kitchen. She finally looks at me. And looks away. As if to say, 'why isn't she doing it?'

"Elizabeth. Is everything okay?" I ask sarcastically. Because frankly. I couldn't give a flying fuck. But I know that there is something wrong with her. She clearly went for a smear test and the nurse put the speculum up her arse instead and left it in there.

She turns her nose up at me. "Where is my granddaughter?" She looks towards Cole again.

Cole looks at me.

I look at him.

Without missing a beat. "Mum. Would you care to acknowledge my beautiful fiancé and mother of my child." Cole folds his arms now, closing his body off.

She sighs.

"It's your father. He's not happy about this arrangement you two have." I'm not sure what she means by 'arrangement'. "You moved in together and had a child and you're not married. You know how we feel about that, Cole." Sorry I didn't realise we were back in the eighteen fucking hundreds. "And we're scared that it's rubbing off on Michelle." I'd hate to tell her that Michelle frequently tells me about her very wild weekends that may or not include controlled substances and a lot of sex with people of all genders.

As much as I disagree with what Elizabeth is saying. I understand. I know how it feels to live your whole life believing something and being so sure of it and not knowing anything different. Then one day everything changes. Elizabeth went to Sunday school, met Cole's dad Samuel at said Sunday school, got married and had three children who were all raised with the same standard that she was. It must be scary for her to realise that her children who she cares for so dearly and taught them everything she knows have grown up and found their own way of life.

"I understand Elizabeth. It's scary." I make my way over to the couch to sit next to her. One of the things I learned in the salon is you have to treat rude people like children. I take her crepey hand in mine which are surprisingly soft *unlike her soul.* "I know how scary it is to have all of these changes happening in your life." I remember the first night Cole and I spent together. We both said it was scary because we weren't sure we were ready to be with anyone. But it was okay because we were scared together. "I didn't think would be my life." Her eyes finally meet mine. I look up at

Cole as he listens intently. "I was certain that I would never fall in love. I didn't know that it existed. And I was terrified when I met Cole." I smile thinking about that time we met in that coffee shop. The blatant confidence that came over him as he swaggered over, but in the same breath he was a nervous wreck. "If I ran away, I wouldn't have found all of the amazing things that have happened." She looks at me more deeply now. Like she now realises that we're not of different teams. "Change can be scary. But it doesn't mean it's a bad thing."

Right on cue, Flora cries over the baby monitor. I let Elizabeth stew for a few seconds. Letting her process everything I said to her. Cole keeps his eyes on me before he shuffles out of the living room to get Flora. "Hello Ophelia." She holds her other hand out to me, her eyes with a hint of emotion behind them. As if what I said hit her in the heart. I don't shake her hand though; Elizabeth and her husband have been awful to me. *And* to Cole. There's no way I'm letting her see Flora if she doesn't apologise. I don't have a problem with having one less person to send a Christmas card to. I grew up with a small family and I don't mind keeping a small family to protect myself, my fiancé and most importantly my daughter. "Ophelia. I'm sorry for how we've treated you… it's just different." Her eyes pleading.

I can hear Cole creep into my office where we Flora down for her nap over the monitor. "It's okay baby. Daddys here. Shhhh." He whispers. God, I love that man.

"Elizabeth. I grew up in a toxic environment. And I got out of it. and I'm not going back into one. And I'm sure as hell not letting Flora grow up in one… So, I will accept your apology. But I will not forget." My words consume her brain. Making her feel things that she didn't think she'd need to.

She takes a deep breath.

"Now. Do you want to meet your granddaughter?" I smile. As if forgetting the years of torment and ignorance. Because right now isn't the time to hold a grudge.

Her eyes become bright and sparkle. Cole has her eyes.

She starts profusely nodding her head, swiping her hands across her face to wipe away the single tear that shed her eyes.

Cole peers behind the door. I nod.

"Hi gran." Cole says, holding Flora in his arms gently, her body wrapped up in her shawl.

Her tears start streaming now. "Oh my, she's beautiful." She exclaims, scooping her up in her arms. Making sure her shawl is properly adjusted round her, so she doesn't get cold.

As much as it has hurt me for the past few years to feel a sense of abandonment and anger at Coles family. And if it were any other circumstances I would have long forgotten about his family. But I'm doing it for Flora. Flora deserves a family. I want her to have the big family dinners that I didn't have.

Cole waves his fingers at me. Ushering me out of the living room. I smile before I head into the hall, slowing down for a moment to admire Flora having something I didn't have.

Cole closes the door to the living room, blocking us in the hallway. "Okay how the fuck did you do that? That was the sexiest thing I've ever witnessed in my life and if you weren't eight days postpartum, I would bend you over right here right now." He laughs.

I laugh too, bringing my fingers up to my face and biting my nails. Coles arms envelope me, each one wrapping round each of my shoulders, my arms reach round his back and pull him in closer. The side of his face pressed into mine. His lips kissing my cheek before he pulls away. Then I pull his lips to mine where they belong.

Chapter 14

I am exhausted. After that deep conversation/telling I had with Elizabeth, my social battery is well and truly drained. I had four different people in my home today. Which was a lot. And I like that I done it in steps. Working my way up to the top level of energy needed. But I could really use a cuddle with my mum right about now. Once Elizabeth left, I took my first shower in three days. I probably should have showered before I had company over. But they weren't here to see me, so it doesn't matter. Cole did walk in while I was showering because Flora wouldn't settle with him, so I just stood wet in the shower with the water off, rocking her until she stopped crying. But all was well in the end.

My hair feels so clean, my legs aren't shaved because I still can't bend down properly because my tummy is still so bloated and sore, that could be a job I could get Cole to do. He has another three weeks off work so he should just about be able to finish weed whacking the forest on my legs before he goes back to work. I'm giving Flora her bedtime bottle. Her mouth suckling on the bottle makes the sweetest noise. I comb my fingers through her short, fine, fluffy hair, admiring all the different shades of brown.

"There's my girls." Cole walks into our bedroom, a towel round his waist and another in his hand, raking it through his hair.

I stray my eyes away from Cole's physique and back to Flora while Cole gets his pyjamas on.

"Can I steal a cuddle from her before she goes to sleep?" He lays on the bed, right in front of me, with his hands on his face like an angel.

"Of course, you can." I smile. I do that a lot now. And I mean it. Passing Flora over to Cole, watching him hold her so passionately yet so softly while she finishes the rest of her bottle.

Cole just finished giving Flora her first night-time bottle. It's midnight. She usually gets up twice through the night for a bottle, around midnight, four then she gets her morning bottle around eight. And Cole takes care of all of them. Even though I usually wake up with him to give him company.

Cole's head hits the pillow again once he puts Flora back down in her basinet at the bottom of our bed. I bring myself closer to him, pulling my arms around him and resting my head on his shoulder.

"Thank you for today." He says in his sleepy voice, his hand tousling my hair. He kisses my forehead softly.

"You don't need to thank me." I say, tracing his jaw with my ring finger.

"No, I do… I'm genuinely so impressed with how you handled her." Cole turns round to face me.

"Well… she's a lot like me." I sit up onto my elbows slightly, wiping my hair out of my face.

"Please don't say that you're like my mother." Cole begs, dragging his hands over his face.

I giggle. "No, I just mean that we're both a bit stubborn… she believed for years that things were wrong. So, I imagine that it would be hard for her to accept things." I say it in such an understanding way when I really don't. I do wish that I met Coles parents earlier on in our relationship. We waited a whole six months. And by that point me and him knew that we were destined for one another. Arguably we knew that after the first date. But we were in it for the long run. When they met me for the first time they asked about my family. Which isn't my favourite topic. They just always treated me like an outsider. Except Michelle. She looks up to me.

I think Michelle could be the sister I didn't know I wanted.

Chapter 15

Waking up to Flora by my side as Cole finishes shaking up the formula. The sloshing waking me from my slumber. I roll over and wrap an arm around Flora. Pulling her closer to me. Taking in every last detail of her. Like how her eyelashes are longer than mine. And how her fingers scrunch up, and the teeny freckle on her right cheek right where her dimples will be.

Cole kisses my forehead before he picks up Flora. I sigh. Stretching my arms out, my eyes finally adjusting to the light. "Good morning beautiful." He says delicately.

“Good morning love.” I say back, still mid-stretch. Dragging myself up and waddling into the bathroom.

I am feeling optimistic today. I *will* wear my adult diaper. But I won’t lace it with aloe vera. My vagina has finally got over the post-partum stage of burning and feeling like it’s going to fall off.

I resume my position on the bed and take my buzzing phone from the bed side table.

Blake- Hi Ophelia. Wow I haven’t text you in a long time. I just wanted to say congratulations. When I ran into you the other week it brought back so much. I was genuinely like a zombie for the next few hours... I was just wondering, do you want to go out for a coffee for a catch up? It’s completely fine if not I just missed talking to you. Wow that makes me sound like a right sap. X

My jaw drops when I read the message. And it surprises me that I feel the same way. Blake was a ginormous part of my life. I want to talk to him. I want to thank him properly.

“Cole.” My voice high pitched.

“Yeah?”

"Are you okay to look after Flora yourself for a few hours? Blake just text me… to go out for coffee." I don't know why but I feel bad about it. I know that I shouldn't though. Although Blake was my first love. And I can't lie to Cole or myself that there isn't any emotional attachment to him. That would be unfair to Blake, not giving him any credit. It is a strange situation. Usually, you don't meet up for coffee with your ex unless you have shared custody of a child or have to warn them of a chlamydia diagnosis. I hate to think that Blake is my 'ex', it's just a thrown to the side way of saying that they were someone you gave a piece of your heart to. But Cole has my whole heart now. And I know that if the shoe was on the other foot, I'd find it weird.

"Of course, I can look after baby Flo myself." He sighs. "If you want to meet up with Blake that is absolutely fine. I won't lie and say that I'm not intimidated. But taking into consideration that you just had my child I *think* I trust you." He laughs it off, but I can tell it makes him uncomfortable.

"You shouldn't be the one intimidated my love." I sit my phone back on my bedside table. Coles looks over at me, scrunching his eyebrows up confused. "Everything you have with me is everything *he* wanted with me."

Walking down this street brings back memories. Like when I would come down here and sneak into my mum's salon during lunch so I wouldn't be a target for the bullies. Walking down here with the anxiety ripping my face apart, sneaking in the back door of the salon to escape. Making noodles in the microwave instead of braving the canteen.

I've got a nail appointment in a few hours, which I think will be well and truly needed after this.

Smiling at the barista before I give her my order. Scanning the coffee shop to see if Blake is here yet. We said we'd meet at ten thirty. It's ten fifteen. "Medium mocha made with oat milk please." I smile again.

"That'll be three pounds eighty pence please." She says with a smile as I rattle around in my purse to get rid of the rest of my change.

"I've got that for her." I hear him say it and my heart skips. I spin round. There he is. Blake. "I'll take a large cappuccino thanks." He says. My dimples showing that I'm happy to see him.

"Hi." My voice croaks. I cover my mouth, clearing my throat. "I'll go get us a table." I say, but I stay standing where I am for a few more seconds. Because I can't believe it. He's actually right in front of me.

Grabbing a handful of sugar and a stack of napkins from the stand I scour the shop for a free table. I head for the low chairs that are too low to sit comfortable in and drink your drink at the same time. Those chairs are made for conversations you don't want people to hear.

Deep breath Ophelia. Deep breath.

The tray hits the table and I'm seventeen. I'm broken. I'm everything that I'm not anymore.

"Congratulations. How's life being a mum?" He asks so nonchalantly, like we see each other all the time and this is just one of our regular catch ups.

"It's scary. But it's good." I sigh, knowing that that's not what he wants to hear. *Deep breath.* "Does your wife know you're with me right now?" I ask blatantly. Because if Blake thinks that this coffee is anything else than coffee, I'm scared I'll break his heart again.

He takes a deep breath. "It was her idea." He admits, picking up his mug. "When I came home that day after seeing you again, I told her everything. I told her how much it hurt me to see you leave me." He puts his cappuccino back on the table after taking a sip. "I didn't tell her much about you. I didn't tell her how much I loved you." I pick up my cup, shaking a sugar packet before I stir it in. "So does your husband know that you're here?" He sits back in his chair.

"Fiancé." I correct. "And yes, he does. He knows all about you. He knows how bad I felt for hurting you. A big chunk of our first date was actually spent talking about you." We go silent for a few seconds. "So, don't tell me you still drive that blue Corsa?" I joke, taking a gulp of my mocha.

He lets out a laugh. "No. Claire was very quick to tell me to get a new one after she found out what we had done in it." I throw my hand over my mouth, almost spitting my drink all down myself. Blake hands me over the stack of napkins. "Here you go." He giggles.

"Thank you." I scrunch up the napkins and throw them back onto the table. Reminiscing on the late night drives we had in that car and 'our spot' and the very not so PG activities that happened there. "When did you become funny?" That's the one thing that Blake never was. He was never funny. It was his one true fault.

"My dad died." The laughing and giggling stop.

I'm left speechless. I try to gurgle up a conjunction of words. But nothing comes out.

"It's okay. It's a good thing. I'm not scared anymore." I think back to that day in my mum's house, he came over hysterically in tears, terrified that his dad was going to hurt his mum again.

"What happened?" I ask, unsure if he wants to answer, or if I even want an answer.

"He was always an alcoholic. He got into drugs apparently. Overdosed." He sighs. "It wasn't how I wanted him to die. I wanted him to hurt like he hurt everyone."

Everything falls silent again.

Since we're on the topic of torture. "Do you remember Dan? Well, I just found out that he battered that guy who hurt me."

"I know."

I scrunch up my face confused.

"He told me after I hurt him too."

Okay is there anyone else in my life that hasn't a secret scuffle with the man who ruined me?

"I lied to you when I told you I didn't know who he was... he was my best friend."

My cup falls to the floor, spilling the rest of the mocha everywhere. I hear the ceramic mug shattering and the stream of the mocha dripping to the floor. Blake rushes to get another stack of napkins.

I'm unable to move while Blake cleans up the mess around me. The barista running over with a roll of blue roll and a cleaning spray, Blakes hands drag me up and out of the way. I stand there frozen. My hands still holding the invisible mug.

"Its's okay, it's safe now." His hands on my forearms sitting me back down.

I try to gurgle more words out. Trying to say too much at once. 'Why didn't you tell me? What did you do? What happened?'

Blake knows me well enough to know that I want and need answers without me having to ask.

"I remember the Monday after the party. I couldn't make it that night because I was working. But that morning I seen the state of him. He had stiches, black eyes, the lot. I asked him what happened. He told me he had sex with someone at the party, he didn't know their name but then the next day their boyfriend started a fight with him… I didn't think much of it to be honest. He was a player, always slept with people he shouldn't, and people would sleep with him when they shouldn't." I can't believe I'm hearing this. A new drink appears like magic.

Brian. Is a fucking monster. He knew he was wrong. He knew what he done was wrong. He didn't even remember my name? Was I that unimportant to him?

"When you told me what happened to you and asked me if I knew him, I said I didn't. I shouldn't have lied. I admit. But at that moment I didn't want to know him. I had to rethink every Monday morning interaction with him. He always bragged about who he seen at the weekend, and I thought 'what if he's been doing it to everyone?' I went home that day and phoned him to meet up at the rugby training grounds. I hadn't played in years." I'm still frozen. Feeling nothing but everything at the same time. "As you can guess I done him in, he never gave me a scratch. He admitted it. I couldn't stop screaming. I was so angry at him. I couldn't understand how anyone could hurt anyone like he did. But especially you. I didn't think anyone was capable of hurting you like he did… he lay on the grounds grunting and I left him there. I phoned Dan and broke down to him. I went over to his and he cleaned me up and I spoke to his mum." He sighs again. "I never heard or spoke to Brian again."

How can so many people have connections to the man that ruined me? Dan invited him to the party, then the next day sent him to hospital, Blake was his *best friend*, then also sent him to hospital. And Cole. He fucking lived with him. And not one of them had a clue of what he was capable of. I guess everyone knows a rapist.

I shake the mug up to my mouth, trembling as I take a sip. "Thank you."

We're silent for a long time. Both of our drinks are finished, and Cole has quietly gone up and ordered more. The cups and plates clinking against the table. "I got you a toastie as well." He slices the knife through it for me and stacks the four triangles across eachother. He remembers that's how I like to eat it. Just like my gran does it.

"Blake. Why did you want to meet up?" I ask the question that I've been wanting to ask since I sat down before the confessions started. Taking a quarter of the toastie in my hand and taking a bite.

Clasping his hands over his face and dragging them down his cheeks. "Do you want me to be honest?"

"That's all I ever want." We're not in a coffee shop anymore, we're in a bubble. It's as if we're in his blue Corsa, in our spot and we've just picked up a takeaway.

Sighing before he starts his sentence. "I wanted to make sure you were okay." He says softly, but with a hint of relief. "I couldn't help it after I saw you on the street. You had things you told me you didn't want. And I wanted to know if you were happy and safe." He says sincerely. "Even though we broke up years ago I still care about you."

I smile down at my mocha, admiring the imperfect coco powder sprinkles. "For the first time ever. I'm doing really good. And I don't need to lie about it." *Deep breath.* "I met Cole in a coffee shop a lot nicer than this one. I fell in love with him right then and there. As much as I loved you all those years ago, this *will* be terrible to hear by the way. But I couldn't love you and love myself at the same time. And that wasn't your fault. I was broken. And I lied to everyone that I wasn't, and you deserved better than that." I lean over the table closer to Blake. His eyes stare into mine. "I found myself and I built her back up. I lost myself in you. My whole world started and ended with you, and I didn't know who I was without you… with Cole." *Deep breath.* Smiling when I say his name. "I love him because I love him. And not because I need to… it took me a long time to realise that I deserve everything that I was holding myself back from…I have a home with a garden, I have a wall in my house dedicated to books, I have a daughter, she is perfect in every way, I have a partner that worships the ground I walk on, calls me beautiful every chance he gets and makes me laugh every day." I start tearing up thinking of all the wonderful things I have that I used to think I didn't want. Now I can't imagine living without them.

Blake sits back in his chair, admiring the words that have just come out of my mouth. "Good. I'm glad." He plays with the words in his mouth, playing with them like bubble gum, like he wants to say something else.

"Are you okay? Are you happy?" I ask, leaning down to take a sip of my now semi-cold drink. "Did you get someone to love you as much as you deserve to be loved?" Sitting the mug back down once the semi-cold mocha touches my lips.

He closes his eyes and smiles. I can only imagine his amazing life by the time he is taking to respond. And for once I'm not jealous or envious. I'm relieved. I think I've spent the past few years worried that he had gave up. Worried that he didn't bother to find love again. I was worried that I had broken him. "She is perfect. Truly." Tapping his fingers together to create the perfect sentence.

"I spent the first few weeks after we broke up in my bed, I took up a new hobby, I learned how to paint. Not very well." He laughs. "I started back at college in the August and I met Claire. It was, I guess you could call it love at first sight." He starts biting his cheek to stop himself from smiling too much. "She was taking some sort of tech course. She now has her degree and to be honest I have no clue what she does because it's too technical for someone who is quote unquote just a barber to understand." He laughs. "We have our beautiful twin babies. We have a home, just down the road from my mum, Claire is an amazing mum, and she tells me every day that I'm a good dad."

"I always knew you'd be."

Me and Blake sit and chat and reminisce for the next hour. We talked about that time we went to the cinema and accidentally walked into the wrong theatre and ended up watching half of the movie before we realised and ran out embarrassed. He teases me about my diary. He never read it, but I carried it everywhere. Or that time when my mum walked in on us in the living room getting freaky. *That was mortifying.* In our defence she was supposed to be out of town all weekend for a beauty convention. And when he convinced me to let him cut my hair and he freaked out and was too scared to ruin my hair.

I check my watch and sigh. I have ten minutes to get to my appointment.

I grab my handbag to get ready to leave. "I hope we can still be friends Blake." I huff, swinging the strap of my bag onto my shoulder.

"Always Ophelia." He shakes his head smiling. We hug before we leave, and it's not a sad hug this time. It's the kind of hug that you give to friends after a coffee catch up. Or the kind of hugs that shows you that you can still love each other and not hurt each other.

Chapter 16

Shutting my car door behind me as I sink into the seat. I didn't tell my mum about seeing Blake. Because then it'll turn into salon gossip, and that's not what I want at all. Admiring my freshly painted pink nails on the steering wheel. Putting my key in the ignition and driving. I go a long drive. I think about all the things that we spoke about. I think about the number of movies we watched on the weekends we spent on my couch. And I try to pinpoint every moment that I lost a part of myself falling in love.

Incoming call- Cole <3

Clicking 'accept' on my dashboard.

"Hi love." I say, wiping away my face because I think I might have been crying.

"Hi, I just wanted to make sure you're okay." He says, Flora crying in the background.

"Yeah, I'm okay. It was just a lot of emotions… I'm just heading back now; I'm taking the country roads to get some air. Do you want me to pick up lunch?" I ask. I don't feel the need to hide anything from Cole. I don't feel the need to hide my emotions from him. Because I know that he'll love me anyway. He'll love me whether I need a drive to collect my feelings or not.

"That would be amazing, because little miss is too distracting to actually make something to eat." I hear her giggling in the background now.

"Okay. I'll be home soon. I love you."

"I love you too Ophelia."

I love them so much. I want to spend the rest of my life feeling how I feel right now. I want to have it all. I can have it all. I can have a job, a partner, a child, friends. I can have love. And I deserve it.

My music blasting in the car, driving carefully down the country roads, windows down and singing my heart out. "Oh Ophelia, you've been on my mind girl since the flood." I haven't listened to this song in years. "Heaven help the fool who falls in love." Pretty sure this song was written about me. I'm hard to love. I know that. I'm complicated, I'm defensive, I'm too independent, I admit that it's hard to love me. I know this because *I* find it hard to love me. But for all of those bad things about me there's ten good ones. I'm passionate, I'm determined, I'm creative, I have an amazing mind and an amazing heart. I'm worthy of everything I thought I wasn't worthy of. I'm hard to love, and that's not a bad thing. All of the so called 'negative things about me aren't so bad, because they make me, me. I need to appreciate all of the so called 'bad' things about me. and I need to learn to love them.

Chapter 17

When I pull into the driveway I see Cole, and Flora in the baby body wrap scarf contraption thing. Smiling instinctively when I see them.

Carrying my handbag and the peri-peri chicken bag up to the door. “Hottest delivery driver ever.” He says. “I am so happy to see you.” He kisses me. My lips kissing his back.

“I love you so fucking much.” I sigh, my shoulders instantly relaxing.

Cole chuckles. “I fucking love you too.” He says, taking the paper bag off me, ushering me in, his hand on my lower back, then closing the door behind us.

The house smells clean. Or like he's just sprayed air freshener to make it smell clean. But no, the washing is hanging outside, the pile of dust I left in the corner is gone. He cleaned. I turn around to face him, still holding Flora. Giving him a child like grin, scrunching my eyes up as a way of saying 'I love you' even though I just said it two minutes ago.

Flora has gone to bed now.

I've taken the rubbish from the takeaway outside to the bin. When I come back in, Cole is folding up the blankets in the living room and blowing out the candles. I've been learning to appreciate the little things about home now, after we put Flora to bed, we clean-up for the night. It's that half an hour of quiet time that can help us keep on top of the housework and all honesty our emotions. I haven't spoken to Cole yet about what me and Blake spoke about. He hasn't asked me. That's another thing I love about Cole. He knows that if I want to talk about something, I will. There's no point in prying.

Making my way into the kitchen to prep Floras bottles I put the kettle on to make myself a cup of tea. Pulling the string of the lavender camomile tea bag out of the cup and around the handle like I always do. Cole walks up behind me, bringing his arms around me, his head resting on my shoulder. He spins me around, so I'm engulfed in his chest, my arms around his neck. Coles hands at my waist, swaying us both side to side, like a sleep deprived ballroom dance. "Are you okay?" He asks, whispering it into my ear, his voice sleepy and muffled by my hair.

Deep breath. "Yeah." My voice full and yet empty. Like I know that there's truth behind it, but I doubt myself. "He was just worried about me."

Cole pulls back, arms still around me though. "What do you mean?"

My forehead falls back to his chest then back up. "I broke up with Blake because he wanted what I have with you. And he wanted to know that I was safe and happy."

Cole takes his hand and tucks stray hairs behind my ear. "And are you?" Holding my head in one hand, still a hand around my waist.

Smiling up at him. "Happier and safer than I ever thought I'd be." I reply. Then he kisses me. And I'm even more happier and safer.

Swaying and dancing in the kitchen until I need to boil the kettle all over again.

Chapter 18

Flora is a month old now. We finally have everything down to a perfect (near perfect) routine. Today is our first proper family outing. We've been to the supermarket and back and forth out walks. But today we're going to a place that will forever hold a special place in mine and Cole's heart.

Our coffee shop.

We haven't been since we moved. It used to be our regular hang out spot. If we were sick of being at home, we would go to our spot. One of the back tables of course. Cole would go up and order us fancy overpriced coffees and cakes. Sometimes we would sit opposite sides of the table from each other and work. But most of the time we would treat it like any other date. We would ask each other quick fire questions. Some of them are silly but a lot of the time we would sit for hours unleashing our darkest most intricate thoughts to each other.

The staff know us here now. We're the 'happy couple'. They noticed that we would go all the time and made sure to always reserve our favourite table if they knew we were going to be there.

When Cole proposed. It was perfect. It was just one of our normal Sunday morning breakfast dates. Cole held the door open for me as normal. Everything looked like it always had. Dim lighting, lamps everywhere, dark oak tables. We took our ordinary seats in the back. Halfway through our coffee and during one of our quick-fire question rounds Cole asked me to marry him. He got down on one knee "Ophelia Opal Bloom. I love you with all my heart. Do you want to not get married with me." I started laughing. Then immediately followed that with a yes. The baristas were all in on it and started applauding and brought out a tray of cakes with sparklers in them and started snapping pictures. The ring is perfect. We had never spoke in length about my want for a certain engagement ring. All I knew was that I didn't want an 'engagement ring' the yellow diamond fits me perfectly. And it has a smaller pink diamond on each side. Anytime I look at it, it makes me smile.

Cole helps carry the pram off the train. Being one stop away from central Glasgow is just close enough for me. I can still say I live in Glasgow. It's as if we're going on a two-week all-inclusive holiday with the amount of stuff we have in Flora's bag. How does a one-month-old need this much stuff?

Holding the door open for me as usual Cole waves at the baristas as I roll in with Flora.

"It's the happy couple. I haven't seen you guys in a while... oh my gosh." He exclaims. Dropping the tea towel on his workstation. I smile giddily when him and the other worker come out from behind the coffee bar to greet us. Telling us congratulations and telling me how amazing she is. Insisting that our drinks are free. Cole sliding money into their tip jar whilst I take our seats.

"Flora my love." I reach into her pram to lift her carefully out, sliding her into my lap. "This is where your mummy and daddy met. Right at this table." I think back to that day a lot. The night before I hadn't got much sleep because I was up late packing orders up. But I still wanted to get up early and get all of my admin work done at one of my favourite coffee shops. My egg and bacon sandwich keeping me company. Coles cute round glasses that I wish he wore more often drew my attention. I asked him if he usually sat with strangers in coffee shops. To which he replied, "Only the pretty ones." That's when I fell in love. If I didn't know it then, I would know it soon.

Looking up from us to see Cole waltzing over with our tray of semi-free coffees and cakes. No cherry bakewell's in sight. "Here you go my girls." I love when he says 'my girls' like he won't let anyone hurt us. He will always protect and nurture us and we will forever be 'his girls' and he will forever be ours. There's no one I want to spend the rest of my life with. Only him. I want to grow old wither that be in our home now or in a care home and we argue constantly because we can't remember anything, and we help each other take our cocktail of pills to keep us functioning. There's no one else I'd rather do that with than Cole. He leaves the table to get the sugar packets that I forgot to lift. But he doesn't make it a big deal.

"Sorry." I say to him once he sits back in his chair, tossing the sugar onto the middle of our table. I'd usually be the one to get them on my way to our table, but I didn't even think to grab them because I was so worried about getting Flora settled.

"Don't be sorry. You have nothing to be sorry for." He assures me, leaning his hand across the table to mine. "I love you." He says.

"I love you too." I smile.

Shaking the sugar packets before putting two of them into my hazelnut latte.

And it's just like one of our normal coffee dates.

Chapter

19

When I was younger, I remember spending all my time reading. I escaped into books. I would spend my nights, mornings, lunch times reading. In primary school in the playground, I would find a corner and hide out until the bell went. Me and Lacy both huddled up each reading quietly. We were called 'wierdos' and 'strange' and we didn't care. Because in our book we were the main characters. We slayed dragons and were wizards. We were so cool.

When Lacy moved schools, I sat myself. And eventually I stopped reading at lunch times. Because without Lacy there I was alone. I then only read at home, or at the salon when I'd go after school. But I pretended that I didn't read for fun, because I didn't want to be alone on the playground anymore. I found a few 'friends', I don't like calling them friends though because they weren't nice people. I felt like I was only friends with them because they could push me around. They said jump, I asked how high? When I got into high school and was praised for my reading and writing skills, they stopped asking me to sit with them at lunch and pretended they didn't know me. I didn't realise at the time, but they were jealous of me. So, I sat alone. For four years. and I wished I kept in touch with Lacy because I know that she would have been sitting next to me reading too.

Lacy is taking her master's degree in physics. She's going into astrophysics. Which would mean that I'd be lying if I said I knew what that was. Something to do with space. I joke that she's an astronaut. We might not see eachother every day, or even every week. But any time she's in town visiting her family or Dan, she comes over. Or most likely we go out shopping. Today's one of the days where we sit in the house. Cole has gone back to work now and sometimes I need a few hours to catch up on work without Flora clinging to me.

All three of us sitting in Self Care Co headquarters, Lacy on the bean bag with Flora on her knee feeding Flora her bottle. I'm sitting at my desk, printing off shipping labels.

"So, I told Dan, listen if you're not going to keep lube in your car, we're not having sex in it." I seriously question the intelligence of this woman sometimes.

I'm taken aback slightly because I honestly wasn't listening to her and have no idea how the conversation got to this.

"Okay. First point. Why can't one of you just bring lube with you? And second. Don't have sex in cars, you're both too old for that shit." I feel more of a mother than a friend. Maybe not mother. Cool aunt. That sounds more acceptable.

She rolls her eyes at me as I stand up to get to my printer.

"I had a coffee with Blake a few weeks ago." I admit. "You remember him, don't you?"

"Oh my god yes. What the fuck? Why?" Lacy starts to stand up now.

"I ran into him before Flora was born. He text me because he wanted to make sure I was okay. So, we went out for a *completely casual* coffee." Flora has finished her bottle now and Lacy has her over her shoulder rubbing her back. "It was just good to see him again and know that we can still be friends."

"I knew Blake in high school. He is a great guy. Even now, I would trust him with my life."'

"Brian was his best friend." I slide the stack of orders onto my work surface.

"Oh, my fuck. So, he was!" Lacy exclaims. "I completely forgot about that… wait. Fuck."

"Yeah. I just found it scary that so many people I love have strings to bad people."

I let the silence between us stew while I pack up orders and shoot content for social media. Lacy quickly breaks the silence by talking about her and Dans sex life. Or lack thereof because of his inability to have lube in his glove box.

"Okay Flora darling. Let's have this house perfect for daddy." I say, sighing as I put a very sleepy Flora into her bouncer for a power nap before Cole gets home. I really enjoy working from home. It gives me a chance to be at work but still keep up to date with my 'routines'. I've always liked having a tidy-ish home. Lived in but not a pigsty. As long as the floors are semi clean and the bins and washing baskets aren't overflowing, I'm happy. Taking the mop and bucket out of the cupboard and getting a sweat on as I whiz around the floors, turning lamps on and big lights off as I go around the rooms, spritzing air freshener and lighting candles as well.

It's the end of Coles first week back at work and he hates it. Well, he loves his work, but he misses not being around me and Flora more. He only works in the office Wednesday through Friday, so he shouldn't really be complaining. He has his little office setup in the dining room for the rare occasion he tries to work from home Monday or Tuesday. Most of the time he just tries to reply to emails during night-time feeds. Which has led to a lot of confused colleagues wondering why he is replying to emails at four in the morning. Cole has worked his way up to senior editor the past year. Which means that he basically tells other editors what to do. He still has a few projects that he works on, mainly authors that worked with him when he first started. He still works mainly in romance; he laughs when I tease him about his love for rom-com novels. And he then teases me because I love them more than him. Although I don't know if I believe him on that.

Michelle has been helping me out a lot with packing orders. I've obviously been paying her. She's still in university, she's studying business and she somehow thinks that I'm qualified enough to consider packing a few orders for me as 'work experience'. *Hey ho I'll take the compliment.* She comes over for a few hours on a Wednesday and Thursday afternoon after her lectures, she says it's to help me out with work and spend time with her niece, but I think she just wants out of her house. Michelle enjoys being here. Around us. Mine and Coles relationship with his family is better than it was however it's never going to be perfect. However, I do think that they like the fact I work from home, it seems more acceptable to them.

I don't think I ever plan on working eighty-hour work weeks like I used to, not on the regular anyways. Once I finally figure out how to start my second book I'll work more, but I don't like considering that work because it's just fun to me.

Dinner is in the oven. Chicken burgers and sweet potato fries. *All frozen of course, who do you think I am?* Flora wakes up just as the clock strikes six and just as Cole's headlights from the car shine in through the windows. I wipe the sweat from my forehead and bend down to pick up Flora, her head rests on my shoulder when I stand back up. Showing me how much she loves me. I kiss the side of her head which luckily still smells of the newborn baby smell. Her hair is coming in now and is the perfect shade of light brown, the perfect concoction of mine and Coles.

Swinging the front door open as Cole slums himself out of his car. Smiling from ear to ear when he sees us. His work bag over his shoulder, rummaging around in it just as the raindrops start to pitter patter onto our cars in the driveway.

"Another one to add to the collection." He chimes, handing me another freshly printed book. Directing us in from the rain as it starts to get heavier. "Ugh." He sighs, sitting his bag at the entrance way table before closing his arms around us both. "I've missed my girls." Kissing Flora on both her cheeks then kissing my lips and groaning again. 'My girls' I love that.

"Did you have a good day?" I smile, taking his hand and dragging him into the kitchen.

"Yeah, it was good, how was yours? The place looks so nice." Cole appreciates the little things like a washing being put away and the floors being swept. And he always makes sure I know that he's noticed the little things. He takes Flora from my arms to have some daddy snuggles, I take a peek in the oven to check on dinner.

"It was great... I think I have the mum boss lifestyle practiced now." Taking an oven glove from the drawer. Cole walks behind the kitchen island now, going into the cupboard to fetch plates. "I just need to get this bloody book wrote." I huff.

"Don't be hard on yourself. Read Well don't have you locked away in a tower. I made it clear to them when you published your first. And honey. I pretty much run the joint now." He clanks away in the cutlery drawer, peering into the oven sneakily to see what's for dinner so he knows what cutlery to get out, because I haven't told him yet.

"I know. But you know what I'm like." Sliding the oven tray out of the oven.

"You'll figure it out don't worry my love." Kissing the side of my head.

Chapter 20

Flora is having her first sleepover tonight. With my mum. "Go and have sex you two." She shouted at us before she ran out of the door. It has been a long and hard three months. And while doctors can *say* six weeks all the live long day, I am here to say. It is not fucking six weeks. Maybe physically six weeks, but mentally, heck no. I was too self-conscious even though I shouldn't be. I sat with my legs open in front of a mirror for collectively hours. I was ashamed when I went into the salon to get waxed last week. My vulva saggy and dull. Cole has assured me that I have nothing to worry about. I haven't even let his see my vagina since I gave birth. As if that didn't scare him off enough.

"Takeaway will be about half an hour." Cole says, planting a kiss on the top of my head from behind the couch. We decided that tonight we would pretend like we're nineteen and twenty-three again. So, we're ordering in a takeaway and pretending like we don't do this at least once a week. But we don't have a child tonight. 'Friends' is cued up on the projector and we are ready for a kid free night.

But oh, I miss her.

"Is it just me that's nervous for tonight?" I ask as I nestle myself onto Cole's chest, his head leaning onto the arm of the couch, his body splayed out the entire length of the couch.

"I know the house feels empty." He sighs, his hand stroking the top of my head.

"Not that." I puff, even though I am nervous for Flora to be with my mum tonight. Even though she was an incredible mother and has watched Flora for us many times, a sleepover is just a bit different. "The expectation to have sex." I say, taking Coles other hand from the back of his head and holding it in my hand, watching and feeling our fingers intertwine.

"My beautiful darling, tonight has no expectations other than a full night's sleep." Leaning down to kiss my head.

"I don't think we'll get much sleep." I tease.

He throws his head back and smiles.

Sitting myself up I straddle myself over his lap, his head coming back up to face me and his hands wandering my thighs, gripping them closer to him.

Our lips crash together, our wandering hands finding new ways to wander, our tongues tangling, Cole sits up more so that our bodies press together closer, one of his hands on my lower back, pulling me closer onto his hips and the other on my neck, his fingers gently pulling on my hair. A mix of panting and moans escape as his lips work their way down my neck. My hands gathering the fabric at the bottom of his shirt, waiting for him to put his hands up before I remove it and toss it to the floor. He does the same with mine. Just as Cole flips me over so he's on top of me…

Knock knock

For fuck sake.

We both sigh disappointed, Cole rushes to the door, practically throwing the twenty pound note out the door. “Do you want to eat just now?” I ask, leaning over from the couch to retrieve my top.

“I know what I’d rather be eating.”

My jaw drops.

The takeaway bag gets thrown onto the kitchen island and I get carried up the stairs, my arms loop around Cole’s neck to feel safer.

He carefully places me in the centre of the bed, kissing me when he lets me go. “Do you want me to get your clothes off?” He whispers, already with his fingers on the waistband of my joggers.

“Yes.” I smile when I say it, appreciating how gentle he’s being.

He glides the joggers down my legs, kissing my thighs as he does so. Carefully edging my knickers down too and throwing them onto the floor. He takes his own clothes off too; I reach around to my bra clasp and undo it.

I feel vulnerable. I haven’t been naked in a sexy way for a while, my body isn’t what it was. My stretch marks have lengthened, and my tummy has more of a pouch now that it did before. I feel ‘mumsy’. Remembering the lingerie that I used to wear just for fun and the dirty texts I would send to Cole to get him riled up. Coles lips plant kisses around my stomach, working his way back up to my lips. "You are beautiful Ophelia. In every way possible." I feel the urge to cover my body up. Which is something I've never felt in front of Cole. He has helped me shower, shaved my legs, looked into my vagina as a head tore through it and yet I'm lying here as Cole kisses me all over and tells me I'm beautiful and I feel insecure.

"I feel insecure." I say, Cole kissing behind my ear.

"My darling. Talk to me." He stops kissing me now and sits up to listen to me.

Deep breath. "My body is different. My vagina is different. And I'm scared that I'm not sexy anymore."

He sighs, his hand gripping my thigh. And I'm suddenly aware that I'm still naked. "Ophelia. you are the sexiest woman I have ever had the privilege of meeting. I find you sexy when you're spotty and covered in sick, you will always be beautiful to me. If you don't want to have sex tonight that is absolutely fine…" His hand finds my hand, holding it tightly. "What can I do to show you that your beautiful?"

"There is one thing that comes to mind." Cole knows what I mean. I don't need to spell it out for him. He kisses the length of my thighs and works magic. Wrapping his arms around my thighs to keep me in place as I squirm. Pulling me closer to him before I explode, holding his hair to keep him from moving until I'm finished.

Oh.

Fuck.

Sadly we couldn't rate the takeaway like we used to.

Chapter 21

6 months later

When me and Cole first started dating, it was getting into the winter, and the Christmas markets were on in Glasgow. We spent way too much time and way too much money at them. Buying mulled wine and getting crepes stuffed with chocolate, then drunkenly and chocolatey comatosely staggering over to the Turkish delight and nut stand and then walked home with a two-kilogram bag of overpriced Turkish delights.

We go to them every year; it was on the way to my apartment, and it lit up St Enoch and George square. But nothing will compare to that first

Christmas season we were together, it was an almost daily occurrence, and we would sing and dance to the music from the speakers and dance in front of the buskers to draw more attention to them so they could make more money. We wrapped ourselves up in hats, scarves and gloves and pictured that we were in a book. The snow would dust the city like icing sugar on our way back home, we would jiggle the key to open the door and spend the night reading snuggled up next to eachother.

We were and *are* so madly in love.

So, in love that no matter how many times we go to the Christmas markets it feels like the first time.

Flora is nine months old now, and as much as she likes to think, she cannot crawl everywhere. It is a mission to strap her into her buggy every time we leave the house. Even though we don't live in central Glasgow anymore I still didn't want to drive. That takes away the specialness of it. Even as a kid we would always get the train. So, we get the train all of one stop. Cole adjusting Flora's jacket and hat at least seven times before we get out of Argyll street station.

The hustle and bustle of Glasgow at Christmas time is unmatched. It's truly magical. The fairy lights flooding Frasers on Buchanan Street, the

Christmas lights going from lamp post to lamp post, cocooning us in a universe of fairy dust.

Wanting to instinctively take the climb up to my old apartment as the cold air hits us. Just to remember how annoying it was to need to lift the door up slightly to unlock it or to see if the new tenants bothered to fix the leaky tap in the bathroom.

Glaring around at the city that I found myself in.

I feel as though I haven't been here for years even though we come here all the time. Me and Cole still come on our dates to the coffee shop we met in, I have book signings at the bookshops and meetings at Read Well. But there's something different about Christmas time.

"Look Flora this is mum and dads favourite place." Cole says, stopping pushing the buggy to lean down to her, adjusting her coat once again to make sure she's warm enough.

Usually, we would come later at night to get the full effect of the lights and the mulled wine but since we have Flora we have come earlier, but still late enough that the sun has set, which isn't saying much since the sun practically sets at four pm in December. Cole turns round to me, adjusting my hat too. "You look so cute in your pink hat." He says kissing me on the cheek. Looping his arm for me to link mine. Resting my head on his shoulder before we start walking again.

First stop- German bratwurst stand. I have always loved this stall. The only way I can describe its appearance is as if a cuckoo clock and a castle had a baby. That's exactly how the stall looks.

I douse mine with sauerkraut. Cole stares at me with disgust. Pushing my sauerkraut covered lips to his and making him laugh.

There was no point in bringing the buggy with us because Cole has not let go of her since we got into the market. I'm glad of it though. It's busy and I'm sometimes scared never mind a nine-month-old. Gripping onto Coles arm whilst I push the empty buggy. Cole brings Flora over to the stall of fake snow whilst I spend the compulsory thirty pounds on rose flavoured Turkish delights. I get them to split in between a few gift boxes to make myself feel better.

I go into just about every stall and stand. Browsing the jewellery and handmade goodies, of course buying something at every one I stop at. Since my business is successful, I like to spread the love. I know when I started Self Care Co every little order made me smile. It still does don't get me wrong.

We get our family pictures taken in the huge inflatable snow globe, smiling stupidly at the photographer that's old enough to be my great grandad, clearly loving his job of watching cheesy couples and children.

"Oh my god we look so ridiculous I love it." Cole laughs, putting the printed picture in his wallet and the keyring on his keys.

My eyes search the crowds as Cole puts Flora back in her buggy before we leave. I smile. And he smiles too. "Blake!" I shout. Blake waves at me. "Cole, I want to introduce you to Blake." I cheer.

Cole takes the buggy from me, letting me rush over. My arms wrap around him, my face in his scarf. "How are you, Ophelia?" He asks grinning cheesily.

"I'm really good." I look behind me to see Cole and Flora standing awkwardly. "Blake, I want you to meet Cole and our daughter Flora." I step back displaying my hands out to display them.

Cole holds his hand out to shake Blakes. "It's so nice to finally meet you, Blake." The sternness and sheer manliness in his voice. I shake my head at him. He coughs. "How are you?" Cole asks Blake in his normal voice.

“I’m really good, just waiting on Claire and the kids, they ran to the pancake stand as soon as we got here.” He chuckles just as they come running up.

“Daddy, we got you the chocolate ones.” Sophie and Jackson look so big now.

“Thank you so much!” He exclaims, taking the paper plate from them. “Do you remember daddies friend Ophelia?” He says. Scooping one of the mini pancakes up and putting it in his mouth whole. “Mhhm, Claire honey. Meet Ophelia and Cole, and Flora.” He moans letting the chocolate take over.

Claire looks exactly how I pictured her. I’ve seen pictures of her on social media of course but she is so graceful. He platinum blonde locks flowing effortlessly over her shoulders.

Her blue eyes find mine and melt away any worries I even had about meeting her. “Ophelia. you absolute darling.” Her arms envelop me. Her sweet perfume comforting me. “I have wanted to meet you ever since Blake told me how amazing you are.” I tuck my hair behind my ears when she releases me. “Huge fan of your book by the way.”

"It's true she has a shrine and sleeps in one of your company t shirts." Blake says, ruffling Sophies hair.

How crazy is it that my ex-boyfriends wife has my book. And sleeps in one of my t-shirts. *That must be interesting in the bedroom.*

She hugs Cole and waves her hand at Flora before ever so ladylike shoving a pancake smothered in syrup into her mouth.

I gulp. Thinking of how amazing everything is. How me and Blake came back from so much tragedy. And we're so happy now. We've both finally found ourselves.

"Well. We better get home before little miss gets too tired. But I can't say enough how nice it was seeing you all." I feel the tears build. I can feel Coles eyes on me smiling as he loops his arm back around mine.

I look around at everyone. Sophie and Jackson's faces covered in chocolate and giggling away to each other.

"It was so amazing to finally meet you, Ophelia. I definitely annoy Blake by talking about your book too much. I can't wait for book two." Claire laughs, holding my hands and shaking them with excitement.

Me, Cole and Flora are dancing in front of the buskers playing and singing Christmas music. Remembering how amazing it is to dance unapologetically.

Falling asleep on Cole's shoulder on the short train journey home.

Tripping in the front door and slamming the Turkish delight boxes on to the kitchen counter for later.

Upstairs we strip each other from our layers, carefully placing an already sleeping Flora into her bed. Kissing her forehead before we switch off the light. "Sleep tight love." I whisper before closing the door, but leaving it open enough for the light in the hall to illuminate the room slightly.

Throwing myself in to the middle of our bed, exhausted from the cold air. Cole crawls onto the bed beside me, draping his hand on my waist. Sighing when his head hits the pillow. "I love you." I say, moving my head over to face him.

"I love you too." He says, pulling me closer to him. "We are going to have the best Christmas ever. We are going to have amazing Christmases from now on okay." His thumb strokes my temples of my forehead.

I nod. "I'd like that."

We fall asleep. The same chocolate comatose state from every year previous. Before we wake up in the middle of the night to get into our pyjamas and of course for a Turkish delight midnight snack.

Chapter 22

My infamous cookies are in the oven, Flora still on the worktop playing with the scraps from the dough. The tree shaped cookie cutters scattered across the kitchen. Both me and Cole covered in flour from head to toe.

We both are off work until the new year. So, we have the better part of two weeks to spend together. I say 'off work' what I mean is that I won't be shipping out orders, I'll still be accepting orders, so by the third of January I will need a warehouse to help me ship out orders. Oh well. That's a problem for another day.

It's Christmas eve so in theory it should be a mad house today. We should be running around like headless chickens looking for wrapping paper and last-minute gifts for people we don't really like. Well for once in my life, it's all done. Presents are all wrapped and were sent to the north pole weeks ago.

Cole went out today and got the last of the Christmas dinner trimmings. The dreaded parsnips. It's going to be our usual over for dinner. My mum, Dan and Lacy. Coles older brother is hosting dinner at his house too and my spidey senses tell me that his mum and dad will have dinner and spend the rest of the night with them. Them and their 'normalness'. *Gross.* Cole is determined to make Christmas dinner all by himself this year. I believe in him, but I do have the number of a Chinese restaurant that is open tomorrow just in case.

Turning on the hot water for Flora's bath time before I leave the kitchen. Leaving the rest of the mess for Cole. Flora giggling as I carry her up the stairs singing "Santa clause is coming to town!" Her sweet, infectious, dopamine inducing laugh bringing even more joy onto my face.

As I run her bath, I get out our matching Christmas pyjamas. The classic red and green tacky as hell stripes and zig zags that should be illegal three hundred and sixty-four days of the year. But somehow are perfect for Christmas. We buy a new pair every year so me and Cole can match and this year we had to hunt far and wide to find a set that has sizes for baby Flora.

Fluffing up the bubbles and plopping her in her bath, watching her face in amazement as the bubbles take over the water. Playing with her toys and giggling away to herself while I wash her.

I can hear Cole downstairs hoovering. To think that I grew up in a household where my mum manically cleaned every Sunday because my dad wouldn't lift a finger to then living with Cole who thrives on late night cleaning sessions. I love him so much.

"Let's get you all ready for Santa baby girl." Lifting her out of the bath and wrapping her in a fresh towel. Waving to the bubbles as Flora watches them go down the drain. Her little hand waving back and forth like the queen.

"Baba." She exclaims. Meaning 'bye bye.'

Turning off Flora's bedroom light, closing the door, but not all the way closed, just enough so there's still light coming in through the hall. "Good night my love." Cole whispers.

Out in the hall I fall into Coles arms. I haven't realised it all night, all December and I probably won't realise it tomorrow. But I am breaking the pattern. I hadn't realised it. But I will be the first woman in my family to fall in love, not out of fear, out of desperation, out of force, but to fall in love because I'm in love. I will be the first woman in my family who celebrates Christmas with happiness and homemade cookies and not alcohol and despair. My daughter will not be another link in the chain. Coles hand on the back of my head and my arms around him. "I love you." I say into his hoodie.

"I love you too my love." He kisses my hair. "Do you want to watch a Christmas movie and eat cookies until Santa comes?" He says. Cole knows that when I feel like this, I'm vulnerable and I probably don't want to talk about it, but what I do want to do is find comfort of the familiarity of Christmas movies. No matter the time of year.

Hot chocolates on the coffee table, the lack of coasters brings me comfort, the not worrying about water rings on the table. Lying on Coles chest, not really watching 'Christmas with the Kranks' but somewhat looking in the direction of the projector screen. "The first Christmas I can remember. I was crying because my dad didn't show up when he said he would." I say. Cole stroking my hair when I say it. I say it so straight faced and to the point, as if I don't think about it a lot and as if it doesn't affect me. When in reality, every time I see a Christmas tree, a stream of tinsel or the twinkling of a light it breaks my heart. It makes me relive it all over again. Standing in my living room, watching out the window, waiting for my dad to pull up. I had a magical morning with my mum and had just finished breakfast, mum made French toast. Dad said he would pick me up at eleven and we would go to his mum's house and open presents and if it was snowing, we would go sledding. I had my hat and gloves on ready to go because I loved sledding. There wasn't much snow on the ground but enough to sled on. My mum tried phoning him for half an hour because she could see how upset I was getting. He didn't answer. She phoned his mum, and I didn't hear what she told her, but I could tell it made my mum angry.

I didn't find out until a few years later that he went out with his friends the night before and didn't get home until six. I was already awake, having an amazing morning with my mum. The first Christmas just us when my so-called dad was getting put to bed by his mother. He didn't pick me up until four. At that point I didn't want to go with him. I wanted to spend the rest of the day with my mum and help her peel potatoes and God-awful parsnips.

He guilted me into going with him. He made me feel as though my feelings were irrelevant and his plans were more important. We ended up at his mum's house after all. I stuck to my gran like glue. She could see how hurt I was. How betrayed I felt because my dad didn't care about me enough to not go out the night before. She drove me home without telling my dad.

My mum got drunk texts from him that night. Telling her it was all her fault. I hate that man. I don't think about my dad a lot. But when I do it's never good. He hasn't spoke to me in almost six years. I'm twenty-three now, I have a fiancé, I have a child, a career and my dad doesn't care. I don't care if he cares though. Because his opinions or thoughts don't matter to me anymore. I hope to God that Flora never has to think that about Cole.

"I'll never show up late. Because I'll always be there. Always. No matter what." He means it when he says it. I know he'll always be here.

He nestles me closer to him, pulling the blanket around us tighter. "I know you'll always be here. And that's why it upsets me." I sigh. Coles looks down at me confused waiting for me to give an explanation. "Why wasn't my dad there? If you can be here, why wasn't he?" I sigh again. Cole tucking hair behind my ear. "I don't care now that he's not. But the point is that he should have been."

"I know baby. I know. But I'm here now. So, you won't ever have to be worried about being disappointed again. As much as you've been hurt in the past. It's in the past for a reason. And I can't wait for more of the future with you." He kisses my forehead for what feels like both the first and millionth time today. Because every time Cole kisses me it feels like the first.

"Let's go to bed. Santa won't come if we're awake." I smile. Putting the thoughts in my head to the side. Pulling Cole off the couch and onto his feet for one more hug. "Race you to bed." I say, pushing him off of me and running up the stairs. But Cole doesn't make an effort to run. Instead, he stays downstairs for a few more seconds. Then he saunters up to find me already tucked into bed. "I won." I cheese.

“What’s your prize?” He asks, jumping into bed beside me.

I look him up and down. Reaching over to him and grabbing his face, pulling him on top of me. *That’s my prize.*

Chapter 23

I wake up to the duvet covers rustling, my hands feel for Cole. “It’s okay I’m here.” He whispers, his hand touching my arm, my eyes still closed and I’m still somewhat asleep, but I can still hear everything. My body finds his and clings to it like a life raft. “Merry Christmas Ophelia.” He kisses my cheek, pulling me into him closer.

There’s something comforting in the fact that it’s Christmas and all I want to do is lay right here. Right here in Cole arms. “Merry Christmas Cole.” I muffle back. My face encased in his chest.

Floras gurgles fall over the monitor. And now I want to be with her. No. I want her to be with us.

Right here. I wish I could teleport her in between us, each of her hands playing with each of our hair, looking at both of us because she doesn't know who she wants to be closer to.

We creak her bedroom door open, my bunny slippers on the wrong feet and my pyjama bottoms rolled up to my knees. Cole's arm around the small of my back. "Merry Christmas Flora." I murmur, putting on her lamp. Her rosy cheeks and green-brown eyes staring back at me. She has pulled herself up onto her feet, clinging to the edge of the cot. Her dummy tossed to the side.

I lift her out, her weight straining my weak morning arms, bringing her into me. Kissing the side of her head. She's sadly lost the new baby smell; she just smells of a perfect mix of me and Cole. Which is even more perfect if you ask me.

We've freshened ourselves all up, fresh nappy, little less BO and a fresh tampon. All three of which are achievements in themselves.

I carry Flora down the stairs on my hip. I never dreamed of carrying my baby on my hip 'so mumsy' I used to say. But I now take 'mumsy' as a compliment. Cole is stepping down behind us.

Pure magic.

It looks like the actual north pole down here. Fake snow, with footprints leading up to the tree, the tree looking fluffier and more sparkly than it did last night. I turn around to Cole. His cheeky grin smiling back at me. "You are incredible." I sigh with happiness.

"I told you that she would never hate Christmas. And you're not going to hate it anymore either." I can't walk. I'm just standing. Here at the bottom of the stairs, looking into the living room at the snowy enchanting haze. "Now hurry up Santa's been." Cole breezes past me, taking Flora from my arms.

I stayed quiet for most of the morning. I don't like opening presents in front of people. I watched as Flora and Cole opened theirs. *Okay Cole helped Flora.* Like what do you even get a nine-month-old for Christmas? She loves soft toys and anything that makes noise. We got here a music set, with a mini xylophone and maracas and a tambourine, which will one hundred percent be getting chucked in the cupboard in about forty-eight hours' time once we're sick of hearing it. And we got her clothes and of course a huge teddy bear that will take up most of the space in her bedroom. I got Cole a ring. He mentioned to me months ago how he wanted an 'engagement ring' because he wanted to make it look 'like he's a taken man' I think he got annoyed with the secretaries at his work for flirting with him if I'm honest. It's just a plain silver band but I had it engraved on the inside with 'Ophelia' and 'Flora' in teeny tiny letters. He started crying when I gave it to him. *Much like the guy at the engraving place.*

I put off opening my present. Because I don't want anything. But Cole insisted. He got me crying too. He had secretly been recording himself throughout the year. Telling me he loves me, how amazing I am, how good of a mum I am. He had it all burned onto a cassette that he wrote- 'For my love. When you need love. Love your love.' On it. He got me a bracelet too, well technically it's from Flora, with an aquamarine gemstone on it to signify her birth month. Over the years there's been two things Cole consistently buys me as gifts, one being of course books, and the other, jewellery. So that anytime he's not around I have a little piece of something to hold onto to, to remind me that I'm not alone.

Chapter 24

This is chaos. Flora is crying because she wants her dad. And her dad is crying because he doesn't know how to tell if the turkey is cooked without cutting it in half.

Shitshow.

That is why I have decided to sit in the bathroom with Lacy and a glass of wine. Nothing a little day drinking and a gossip session with your best friend can't fix. Well, preferably on a beach with hot bar staff, but my guest bathroom with four empty rolls of toilet roll balancing on the cistern will need to do. Dan and my mum are out there, Dan trying to control Flora from not crawling out of sight and my mum is going between them and Cole to try and sort out dinner. "You know my parents are having dinner at their house, we could just escape, and they'd never know we were gone." Lacy teases. "But my dad refuses to serve actual Christmas dinner so that why I always come here." She gulps down the rest of the wine in her glass.

I laugh. I've been doing that a lot today. Laughing. Not at anything in particular though. I'm just laughing because I can.

Hearing a clatter from the kitchen I sigh. "Okay let's go see what's happening." I say, my knees clicking as I stand up from the toilet. Lacy pulling herself up using the towel rail.

Everything is paused when we get to the kitchen. Like it's a movie and someone paused it so they could go to the loo. Mum, Dan, Cole, even Flora, all as still as statues. Mum has her hands over her mouth, Cole has his hands in his hair and Dan is Holding Flora straight out in front of him. "What's happened?" I huff. Strutting over to where everyone is looking, behind the kitchen island I see it. The turkey. On the ground. With the glass dish it was cooked in smashed to smithereens, the turkey juices spreading across the floor. *The parsnips sadly intact on the worktop.* "I'll phone the Chinese."

"That would be brilliant. Thank you." Cole starts down at his dishevelled, prize possession turkey, almost tearing up at all his hard work.

"Clean that up before I come back here."

This is turning out to be a pretty good Christmas.

With enough food to feed the whole of Glasgow sprawled out on the island we each dig in, spoonful's laden with noodles and various salt and chilli concoctions. The mountain of prawn crackers fits nicely on the dinner table where the turkey would have gone. Cole still butthurt at his failed attempt at diner. Me extremely happy that I got my way. Flora is sitting in her highchair next to my mum, playing with her forkful of noodles.

"Well, everyone. Thank you for coming. Dig in." I sigh, noticing Dan already started eating his spareribs.

I hope he never changes. I hope nothing ever changes. I want us all to remain here. All the people I love right here, around this table. I sit still with my cutlery in my hands admiring everyone.

My mum is next to me, then Flora next to her, at the other side of the table it's Dan, Lacy and Cole. All tucking into their long-awaited dinner. Coles foot touches mine. "Are you okay?" He mouths.

"I love you." I whisper.

"I love you too." Our feet still touching, just like our first date.

Chapter 25

Everyone has gone home for the night. Me and Cole cleaned up all the dishes and shreds of wrapping paper, playing Christmas music in the background, like we've done every year since we met.

I'm waiting for the milk to finish warming to make us hot chocolates. I hear Cole talking to Flora in the living room. "What Christmas movie do you want to watch baby?" He clicks the laptop on and picks one. I love overhearing little bits of his conversations with her. "Okay let's watch 'home alone' that's one of mummy's favourites." The microwave dings and I mix the coco powder into the milk. Swirling the whipped cream on top. Of course, adding mini marshmallows and sliding in a candy cane. It is Christmas after all.

Teetering around the trail of toys and cosy blankets to reach the living room. Sitting the mugs onto the coffee table. “Thank you darling.” Cole says, kissing my cheek whilst Flora lunges herself over to me. It’s crazy to me that she’s nine months old now. She lands in my arms and wraps herself around me.

“I love you so much my baby girl.” I whisper into her ears. Kissing her cheek before Cole leans over to us both, encasing us in his arms.

“I’m so happy I have you both.” He grins, pulling us both onto him. Smothering us in his love.

Flora is on the floor now, with Cole. *Of course.* Playing with some of the new toys she got for Christmas. Kevin is back from the church and his mac and cheese is in the microwave. I browse around the living room, the blinds are drawn, the lamps are on, candles lit. My eyes stop at the Christmas tree, and the one ornament that makes my heart melt. The one of a mum, dad and a baby each with our names on it. It finally made its way back to me. The ornament that broke my heart when I was eight. I didn’t put it there. I don’t remember buying it. “Cole, where did that ornament come from?" I ask, pulling his attention away from Floras building blocks.

He smiles at me. And then looks at the ornament. "I remember that you told me that you had one when you were a kid... I wanted Flora to have one. I completely forgot I bought it at the Christmas market, and I found it last night." He says, looking up at me from the floor.

I rise from the couch, my knees cracking when my fluffy socks hit the floor. The twinkly lights brightening up my face. I take the ornament in my hand, playing with the ribbon that is looped around the tree branch. Cole stands up too, picking up Flora when he does. Holding the ornament when Cole wraps an arm around me. "Thank you... for everything."

Chapter 26

My laptop on my knees, Flora safe and sound in bed and Cole in the kitchen putting the dishes away. I know what I'm writing now.

I don't know how I'm supposed to start this. I've went back and forth in my head for what feels like forever about what I want this book to be about. And I know 'well don't write one if you don't want to write one'. But what people don't understand is that when I wrote my first book, I helped so many people. And now it's time to help myself. So here it is. The diary of Ophelia Bloom. Now I'm not going to write about what I ate for lunch or what I wore on the second of February 2013. I'm going to write about how I overcame myself.

And how I learned to love myself when I thought no one could.

Epilogue

Four years later

It's been four years since Ophelia Bloom published her second novel.

She, Cole and Flora still live in their three-bedroom home on the outskirts of Glasgow. Ophelia spends her days writing. She has been featured in many news articles after her novel stirred the pot. She ended up being a guest on a few daytime television shows where she spoke about overcoming trauma and learning to love yourself when you grew up hating yourself. Cole is now one of the company directors for Read Well publishing, and with his promotion he was able to work from home and choose his own hours. He made the case that his fiancé was an 'A lister' and needed to work around her. Lacy graduated top of her class and works for a university astrophysics department. Dan graduated university too, with a little help from Lacy of course. He started working in his mum's office and with a little TLC he's going to become a great lawyer. Cherry has retired early. Which is something she never thought she would do. She still pops into the salon every week to see the girls that she practically raised. Flora starts school next year. She is the sweetest, most caring little girl. Her nursery teacher asked her what she wanted to be when she grew up. She replied 'my mum'.

Acknowledgements

Wow. Okay.

How do you write these?

I want to say a massive, humongous, catastrophic thank you to everyone who read the first book in this duology 'Love Lia xox', those of you who sat across from me at my desk and unleashed your love of it. I didn't intend of writing a second book. I knew what I would want to happen, and I left it at that. And then you guys told me you wanted another. So here ya go.

Writing has always been an escape for me. Like when I wrote a novella in high school, I lived it, I breathed it. And for a long time, I thought it would be my little thing that I wouldn't tell anyone about, and I'm so glad I told people and now I have the chance to share parts of my heart with all you amazing people.

My amazing friend Lukas for doing my covers and also for being someone I can always count on. CFI agents for life. I love you.

When I started writing 'Love Lia xox' I didn't think many people would read it. Or that many people would be interested in little old me. Writing is a way for me to process my feelings. And my clients will tell you that I'm in a hundred different places at once, so it feels good to just be *in* a story.

I started writing 'Love Lia xox' because I was lying in bed and didn't think love existed. And now I do. And I hope you do to.

Because everyone deserves a love they read about in books.

Printed in Great Britain
by Amazon